P. G. Wodehouse

'The ultimate in comfort reading because nothing bad ever happens in P.G. Wodehouse land. Or even if it does, it's always sorted out by the end of the book. For as long as I'm immersed in a P.G. Wodehouse book, it's possible to keep the real world at bay and live in a far, far nicer, funnier one where happy endings are the order of the day' *Marian Keyes*

'You should read Wodehouse when you're well and when you're poorly; when you're travelling, and when you're not; when you're feeling clever, and when you're feeling utterly dim. Wodehouse always lifts your spirits, no matter how high they happen to be already' *Lynne Truss*

'P.G. Wodehouse remains the greatest chronicler of a certain kind of Englishness, that no one else has ever captured quite so sharply, or with quite as much wit and affection' *Julian Fellowes*

'Not only the funniest English novelist who ever wrote but one of our finest stylists. His world is perfect, his stories are perfect, his writing is perfect. What more is there to be said?' *Susan Hill*

'One of my (few) proud boasts is that I once spent a day interviewing P.G. Wodehouse at his home in America. He was exactly as I'd expected: a lovely, modest man. He could have walked out of one of his own novels. It's dangerous to use the word genius to describe a writer, but I'll risk it with him' *John Humphrys*

'The incomparable and timeless genius – perfect for readers of all ages, shapes and sizes!'

'A genius . . . Elusive, delicate but lasting. He created such a credible world that, sadly, I suppose, never really existed but what a delight it always is to enter it and the temptation to linger there is sometimes almost overwhelming' *Alan Ayckbourn*

'Wodehouse was quite simply the Bee's Knees. And then some' *Joseph Connolly*

'Compulsory reading for anyone who has a pig, an aunt – or a sense of humour!' *Lindsey Davis*

'I constantly find myself drooling with admiration at the sublime way Wodehouse plays with the English language' *Simon Brett*

'I've recorded all the Jeeves books, and I can tell you this: it's like singing Mozart. The perfection of the phrasing is a physical pleasure. I doubt if any writer in the English language has more perfect music' *Simon Callow*

'Quite simply, the master of comic writing at work' *Jane Moore*

'To pick up a Wodehouse novel is to find oneself in the presence of genius – no writer has ever given me so much pure enjoyment' *John Julius Norwich*

'P.G. Wodehouse is the gold standard of English wit' *Christopher Hitchens*

'Wodehouse is so utterly, properly, simply funny' *Adele Parks*

'To dive into a Wodehouse novel is to swim in some of the most elegantly turned phrases in the English language' *Ben Schott*

'P.G. Wodehouse should be prescribed to treat depression. Cheaper, more effective than valium and far, far more addictive' *Olivia Williams*

'My only problem with Wodehouse is deciding which of his enchanting books to take to my desert island' *Ruth Dudley Edwards*

The author of almost a hundred books and the creator of
Jeeves, Blandings Castle, Psmith, Ukridge, Uncle Fred and
Mr Mulliner, P.G. Wodehouse was born in 1881 and educated
at Dulwich College. After two years with the Hong
Kong and Shanghai Bank he became a full-time writer,
contributing to a variety of periodicals including *Punch*
and the *Globe*. He married in 1914. As well as his novels
and short stories, he wrote lyrics for musical comedies
with Guy Bolton and Jerome Kern, and at one time had
five musicals running simultaneously on Broadway. His time in
Hollywood also provided much source material for fiction.

At the age of 93, in the New Year's Honours List of 1975,
he received a long-overdue knighthood, only to die
on St Valentine's Day some 45 days later.

P.G. Wodehouse titles available from Arrow

JEEVES

The Inimitable Jeeves
Carry On, Jeeves
Very Good, Jeeves
Thank You, Jeeves
Right Ho, Jeeves
The Code of the Woosters
Joy in the Morning
The Mating Season
Ring for Jeeves
Jeeves and the Feudal Spirit
Jeeves in the Offing
Stiff Upper Lip, Jeeves
Much Obliged, Jeeves
Aunts Aren't Gentlemen

BLANDINGS

Something Fresh
Leave it to Psmith
Summer Lightning
Blandings Castle
Uncle Fred in the Springtime
Full Moon
Pigs Have Wings
Service with a Smile
A Pelican at Blandings

MULLINER

Meet Mr Mulliner
Mulliner Nights
Mr Mulliner Speaking

UNCLE FRED

Cocktail Time
Uncle Dynamite

GOLF

The Clicking of Cuthbert
The Heart of a Goof

OTHERS

Piccadilly Jim
Ukridge
The Luck of the Bodkins
Laughing Gas
A Damsel in Distress
The Small Bachelor

Hot Water
Summer Moonshine
The Adventures of Sally
Money for Nothing
The Girl in Blue
Big Money
Young Men in Spats

Service with a Smile

CHAPTER ONE

I

The morning sun shone down on Blandings Castle, and the various inmates of the ancestral home of Clarence, ninth Earl of Emsworth, their breakfasts digested, were occupying themselves in their various ways. One may as well run through the roster just to keep the record straight.

Beach, the butler, was in his pantry reading an Agatha Christie; Voules, the chauffeur, chewing gum in the car outside the front door. The Duke of Dunstable, who had come uninvited for a long visit and showed no signs of ever leaving, sat spelling through *The Times* on the terrace outside the amber drawing-room, while George, Lord Emsworth's grandson, roamed the grounds with the camera which he had been given on his twelfth birthday. He was photographing – not that the fact is of more than mild general interest – a family of rabbits down by the west wood.

Lord Emsworth's sister, Lady Constance, was in her boudoir writing a letter to her American friend James Schoonmaker. Lord Emsworth's secretary, Lavender Briggs, was out looking for Lord Emsworth. And Lord Emsworth himself, accompanied by Mr Schoonmaker's daughter Myra, was on his way to the headquarters of Empress of Blandings, his pre-eminent sow, three times silver medallist in the Fat Pigs class at the Shropshire Agricultural Show. He had taken the girl with him because it seemed to him that she was a trifle on the low-spirited side these days, and he knew from his own experience that there was nothing like an after-breakfast look at the Empress for bracing one up and bringing the roses back to the cheeks.

'There is her sty,' he said, pointing a reverent finger as they crossed the little meadow dappled with buttercups and daisies. 'And that is my pigman Wellbeloved standing by it.'

Myra Schoonmaker, who had been walking with bowed head, as if pacing behind the coffin of a dear and valued friend, glanced listlessly in the direction indicated. She was a pretty girl of the small, slim, slender type, who would have been prettier if she had been more cheerful. Her brow was furrowed, her lips drawn, and the large brown eyes which rested on George Cyril Wellbeloved had in them something of the sadness one sees in those of a dachshund which, coming to the dinner table to get its ten per cent, is refused a cut off the joint.

'Looks kind of a plugugly,' she said, having weighed George Cyril in the balance.

'Eh? What? What?' said Lord Emsworth, for the word was new to him.

'I wouldn't trust a guy like that an inch.'

Enlightenment came to Lord Emsworth.

'Ah, you have heard, then, how he left me some time ago and went to my neighbour, Sir Gregory Parsloe. Outrageous and disloyal, of course, but these fellows will do these things. You don't find the old feudal spirit nowadays. But all that is in the past, and I consider myself very fortunate to have got him back. A most capable man.'

'Well, I still say I wouldn't trust him as far as I can throw an elephant.'

At any other moment it would have interested Lord Emsworth to ascertain how far she could throw an elephant, and he would have been all eager questioning. But with the Empress awaiting him at journey's end he was too preoccupied to go into the matter. As far as he was capable of hastening, he hastened on, his mild eyes gleaming in anticipation of the treat in store.

Propping his back against the rail of the sty, George Cyril Wellbeloved watched him approach, a silent whistle of surprise on his lips.

'Well, strike me pink!' he said to his immortal soul. 'Cor chase my aunt Fanny up a gum tree!'

What had occasioned this astonishment was the fact that his social superior, usually the sloppiest of dressers and generally regarded as one of Shropshire's more prominent eyesores, was now pure Savile Row from head to foot. Not even the *Tailor and Cutter's* most acid critic could have found a thing to cavil at in the quiet splendour of his appearance. Enough to startle any beholder accustomed to seeing him in baggy flannel trousers, an old shooting coat with holes in the elbows, and a hat which would have been rejected disdainfully by the least fastidious of tramps.

It was no sudden outbreak of foppishness that had wrought this change in the ninth earl's outer crust, turning him into a prismatic sight at which pigmen blinked amazed. As he had explained to Myra Schoonmaker on encountering her mooning about in the hall, he was wearing the beastly things because he was going to London on the 10.35 train, because his sister Connie had ordered him to attend the opening of

Parliament. Though why Parliament could not get itself opened without his assistance he was at a loss to understand.

A backwoods peer to end all backwoods peers, Lord Emsworth had a strong dislike for London. He could never see what pleasure his friend Ickenham found in visiting that frightful city. The latter's statement that London brought out all the best in him and was the only place where his soul could expand like a blossoming flower and his generous nature find full expression bewildered him. Himself he wanted nothing but Blandings Castle, even though his sister Constance, his secretary Lavender Briggs and the Duke of Dunstable were there and Connie, overriding his veto, had allowed the Church Lads' Brigade to camp out by the lake. Many people are fond of church lads, but he was not of their number, and he chafed at Connie's highhandedness in letting loose on his grounds and messuages what sometimes seemed to him about five hundred of them, all squealing simultaneously.

But this morning there was no room in his mind for morbid thoughts about these juvenile pluguglies. He strongly suspected that it was one of them who had knocked his top hat off with a crusty roll at the recent school treat, but with a visit to the Empress in view he had no leisure to brood of past wrongs. One did not think of mundane things when about to fraternize with that wonder-pig.

Arriving at her G.H.Q., he beamed on George Cyril Wellbeloved as if on some spectacle in glorious technicolor. And this was odd, for the O.C. Pigs, as Myra Schoonmaker had hinted, was no feast for the eye, having a sinister squint, a broken nose acquired during a political discussion at the Goose and Gander in Market Blandings, and a good deal of mud all over him. He also smelt rather strongly. But what enchanted Lord Emsworth, gazing on this son of the soil, was not his looks or the bouquet he diffused but his mere presence. It thrilled him to feel that this prince of pigmen was back again, tending the Empress once more. George Cyril might rather closely resemble someone for whom the police were spreading a drag-net in the expectation of making an arrest shortly, but nobody could deny his great gifts. He knew his pigs.

So Lord Emsworth beamed, and when he spoke did so with what, when statesmen meet for conferences, is known as the utmost cordiality.

'Morning, Wellbeloved.'

'Morning, m'lord.'

'Empress all right?'

'In the pink, m'lord.'

'Eating well?'

'Like a streak, m'lord.'

'Splendid. It is so important,' Lord Emsworth explained to Myra Schoonmaker, who was regarding the noble animal with a dull eye, 'that her appetite should remain good. You have of course read your Wolff-Lehmann and will remember that, according to the Wolff-Lehmann feeding standards, a pig, to enjoy health, must consume daily nourishment amounting to fifty-seven thousand eight hundred calories, these to consist of proteids four pounds five ounces, carbohydrates twenty-five pounds.'

'Oh?' said Myra.

'Linseed meal is the secret. That and potato peelings.'

'Oh?' said Myra.

'I knew you would be interested,' said Lord Emsworth. 'And of course skimmed milk. I've got to go to London for a couple of nights, Wellbeloved. I leave the Empress in your charge.'

'Her welfare shall be my constant concern, m'lord.'

'Capital, capital, capital,' said Lord Emsworth, and would probably have gone on doing so for some little time, for he was a man who, when he started saying 'Capital', found it hard to stop, but at this moment a new arrival joined their little group, a tall, haughty young woman who gazed on the world through harlequin glasses of a peculiarly intimidating kind. She regarded the ninth earl with the cold eye of a governess of strict views who has found her young charge playing hooky.

'Pahdon me,' she said.

Her voice was as cold as her eye. Lavender Briggs disapproved of Lord Emsworth, as she did of all those who employed her, particularly Lord Tilbury of the Mammoth Publishing Company, who had been Lord Emsworth's predecessor. When holding a secretarial post, she performed her duties faithfully, but it irked her to be a wage slave. What she wanted was to go into business for herself as the proprietress of a typewriting bureau. It was the seeming impossibility of ever obtaining the capital for this venture that interfered with her sleep at night and in the daytime made her manner more than a little forbidding. Like George Cyril Wellbeloved, whose views were strongly communistic, which was how he got that broken nose, she eyed the more wealthy of her circle askance. Idle rich, she sometimes called them.

Lord Emsworth, who had been scratching the Empress's back with the ferrule of his stick, an attention greatly appreciated by the silver medallist, turned with a start, much as the Lady of Shalott must have turned when the curse came upon her. There was always something about his secretary's voice, when it addressed him unexpectedly, that gave him the feeling that he was a small boy again and had been caught by the authorities stealing jam.

'Eh, what? Oh, hullo, Miss Briggs. Lovely morning.'

'Quate. Lady Constance desiah-ed me to tell you that you should be getting ready to start, Lord Emsworth.'

'What? What? I've plenty of time.'

'Lady Constance thinks othahwise.'

'I'm all packed, aren't I?'

'Quate.'

'Well, then.'

'The car is at the door, and Lady Constance desiah-ed me to tell you –'

'Oh, all right, all right,' said Lord Emsworth peevishly, adding a third 'All right' for good measure. 'Always something, always something,' he muttered, and told himself once again that, of all the secretarial assistants he had had, none, not even the Efficient Baxter of evil memory, could compare in the art of taking the joy out of life with this repellent female whom Connie in her arbitrary way had insisted on engaging against his strongly expressed wishes. Always after him, always harrying him, always popping up out of a trap and wanting him to *do* things. What with Lavender Briggs, Connie, the Duke and those beastly boys screaming and yelling beside the lake, life at Blandings Castle was becoming insupportable.

Gloomily he took one last, lingering look at the Empress and pottered off, thinking, as so many others had thought before him, that the ideal way of opening Parliament would be to put a bomb under it and press the button.

2

The Duke of Dunstable, having read all he wanted to read in *The Times* and given up a half-hearted attempt to solve the crossword puzzle, had left the terrace and was making his way to Lady Constance's sitting-room. He was looking for someone to talk to, and Connie, though in his opinion potty, like all women, would be better than nothing.

He was a large, stout, bald-headed man with a jutting nose, prominent eyes and a bushy white moustache of the type favoured by regimental sergeant majors and walruses. In Wiltshire, where he resided when not inviting himself for long visits to the homes of others, he was far from popular, his standing among his neighbours being roughly that of a shark at a bathing resort – something, that is to say, to be avoided on all occasions as nimbly as possible. A peremptory manner and an autocratic disposition combined to prevent him winning friends and influencing people.

He reached his destination, went in without knocking, found Lady Constance busy at her desk, and shouted 'Hoy!'

The monosyllable, uttered in her immediate rear in a tone of voice usually confined to the hog-calling industry of western America, made Lady Constance leap like a rising trout. But she was a hostess. Concealing her annoyance, not that that was necessary, for her visitor since early boyhood had never noticed when he was annoying anyone, she laid down her pen and achieved a reasonably bright smile.

'Good morning, Alaric.'

'What do you mean, good morning, as if you hadn't seen me before today?' said the Duke, his low opinion of the woman's intelligence confirmed. 'We met at breakfast, didn't we? Potty thing to say. No sense to it. What you doing?'

'Writing a letter.'

'Who to?' said the Duke, never one to allow the conventions to interfere with his thirst for knowledge.

'James Schoonmaker.'

'Who?'

'Myra's father.'

'Oh, yes, the Yank I met with you in London one day,' said the Duke, remembering a tête-à-tête luncheon at the Ritz which he had joined uninvited. 'Fellow with a head like a pumpkin.'

Lady Constance flushed warmly. She was a strikingly handsome woman, and the flush became her. Anybody but the Duke would have seen that she resented this loose talk of pumpkins. James Schoonmaker was a very dear friend of hers, and she had sometimes allowed herself to think that, had they not been sundered by the seas, he might one day have become something more. She spoke sharply.

'He has not got a head like a pumpkin!'

'More like a Spanish onion, you think?' said the Duke, having weighed this. 'Perhaps you're right. Silly ass, anyway.'

Lady Constance's flush deepened. Not for the first time in an association which had lasted some forty years, starting in the days when she had worn pigtails and he had risked mob violence by going about in a Little Lord Fauntleroy suit, she was wishing that her breeding did not prohibit her from bouncing something solid on this man's bald head. There was a paper-weight at her elbow which would have fitted her needs to a nicety. Debarred from physical self-expression by a careful upbringing at the hands of a series of ladylike governesses, she fell back on hauteur.

'Was there something you wanted, Alaric?' she asked in the cold voice which had so often intimidated her brother Clarence.

The Duke was less susceptible to chill than Lord Emsworth. Coldness in other people's voices never bothered him. Whatever else he had been called in the course of his long life, no one had ever described him as a sensitive plant.

'Wanted someone to talk to. Seems impossible to find anyone to talk to in this blasted place. Not at all sure I shall come here again. I tried Emsworth just now, and he just yawped at me like a half-wit.'

'He probably didn't hear you. You know how dreamy and absent-minded Clarence is.'

'Dreamy and absent-minded be blowed! He's potty!'

'He is not!'

'Of course he is. Do you think I don't know pottiness when I see it? My old father was potty. So was my brother Rupert. So are both my nephews. Look at Ricky. Writes poetry and sells onion soup. Look at Archie. An artist. And Emsworth's worse than any of them. I tell you he just yawped at me without uttering, and then he went off with that girl Clarissa Stick-in-the-mud.'

'Myra Schoonmaker.'

'Same thing. She's potty, too.'

'You seem to think everybody potty.'

'So they are. Very rare to meet anyone these days with the intelligence of a cockroach.'

Lady Constance sighed wearily.

'You may be right. I know so few cockroaches. What makes you think that Myra is mentally deficient?'

'Can't get a word out of her. Just yawps.'

Lady Constance frowned. She had not intended to confide her young guest's private affairs to a man who would probably spread them far and near, but she felt that the girl's reputation for sanity should be protected.

'Myra is rather depressed just now. She has had an unfortunate love affair.'

This interested the Duke. He had always been as inquisitive as a cat. He blew his moustache up against his nose and allowed his eyes to protrude.

'What happened? Feller walk out on her?'

'No.'

'She walk out on him?'

'No.'

'Well, somebody must have walked out on someone.'

Lady Constance felt that having said so much she might as well tell all. The alternative was to have the man stand there asking questions for the rest of the morning, and she wanted to finish her letter.

'I put a stop to the thing,' she said curtly.

The Duke gave his moustache a puff.

'You did? Why? None of your ruddy business, was it?'

'Of course it was. When James Schoonmaker went back to America, he left her in my charge. I was responsible for her. So when I found that she had become involved with this man, there was only one thing to do, take her away to Blandings, out of his reach. He has no money, no prospects, nothing. James would never forgive me if she married him.'

'Ever seen the chap?'

'No. And I don't want to.'

'Probably a frightful bounder who drops his aitches and has cocoa and bloaters for supper.'

'No, according to Myra, he was at Harrow and Oxford.'

'That damns him,' said the Duke, who had been at Eton and Cambridge. 'All Harrovians are the scum of the earth, and Oxonians are even worse. Very wise of you to remove her from his clutches.'

'So I thought.'

'That's why she slinks about the place like a funeral mute, is it? You ought to divert her mind from the fellow, get her interested in somebody else.'

'The same idea occurred to me. I've invited Archie to the castle.'

'Archie who?'

'Your nephew Archie.'

'Oh, my God! That poop?'

'He is not a poop at all. He's very good-looking and very charming.'

'Who did he ever charm? Not me.'

'Well, I am hoping he will charm her. I'm a great believer in propinquity.'

The Duke was not at his best with long words, but he thought he saw what she was driving at.

'You mean if he digs in here, he may cut this bloater-eating blighter out? Girl's father's a millionaire, isn't he?'

'Several times over, I believe.'

'Then tell young Archie to get after the wench with all speed,' said the Duke enthusiastically. His nephew was employed by the Mammoth Publishing Company, that vast concern which supplies the more fatheaded of England's millions with their daily, weekly and monthly reading matter, but in so minor a capacity that he, the Duke, was still obliged to supplement his salary with an allowance. And if there was one thing that parsimonious man disliked, it was supplementing people's salaries with allowances. The prospect of getting the boy off his payroll was a glittering one, and his eyes bulged brightly as he envisaged it. 'Tell him to spare no effort,' he urged. 'Tell him to pull up his socks and leave no stone unturned. Tell him – Oh, hell! Come in, curse you.'

There had been a knock at the door. Lavender Briggs entered, all spectacles and efficiency.

'I found Lord Emsworth, Lady Constance, and told him the car was in readiness.'

'Oh, thank you, Miss Briggs. Where was he?'

'Down at the sty. Would there be anything furthah?'

'No thank you, Miss Briggs.'

As the door closed, the Duke exploded with a loud report.

'Down at the sty!' he cried. 'Wouldn't you have known it! Whenever you want him, he's down at the sty, gazing at that pig of his, absorbed, like somebody watching a strip-tease act. It's not wholesome for a man to worship a pig the way he does. Isn't there something in the Bible about the Israelites worshipping a pig? No, it was a golden calf, but the principle's the same. I tell you . . .'

He broke off. The door had opened again. Lord Emsworth stood on the threshold, his mild face agitated.

'Connie, I can't find my umbrella.'

'Oh, Clarence!' said Lady Constance with the exasperation the head of the family so often aroused in her, and hustled him out towards the cupboard in the hall where, as he should have known perfectly well, his umbrella had its home.

Left alone, the Duke prowled about the room for some moments, chewing his moustache and examining his surroundings with popping eyes. He opened drawers, looked at books, stared at pictures, fiddled with pens and paper-knives. He picked up a photograph of Mr Schoonmaker and thought how right he had been in comparing his head to a pumpkin. He read the letter Lady Constance had been writing. Then, having exhausted all the entertainment the room had to offer, he sat down at the desk and gave himself up to thoughts of Lord Emsworth and the Empress.

Every day in every way, he was convinced, association with that ghastly porker made the feller pottier and pottier. And, in the Duke's opinion, he had been quite potty enough to start with.

3

As the car rolled away from the front door, Lord Emsworth inside it clutching his umbrella, Lady Constance stood drooping wearily with the air of one who has just launched a battleship. Beach, the butler, who had been assisting at his employer's departure, eyed her with respectful sympathy. He, too, was feeling the strain that always resulted from getting Lord Emsworth off on a journey.

Myra Schoonmaker appeared, looking, except that she was not larded with sweet flowers, like Ophelia in Act Four, Scene Five, of Shakespeare's well-known play *Hamlet*.

'Oh, hello,' she said in a hollow voice.

'Oh, there you are, my dear,' said Lady Constance, ceasing to be the battered wreck and becoming the hostess. 'What are you planning to do this morning?'

'I don't know. I might write a letter or two.'

'I have a letter I must finish. To your father. But wouldn't it be nicer to be out in the open on such a lovely day?'

'Oh, I don't know.'

'Why not?'

'Oh, I don't know.'

Lady Constance sighed. But a hostess has to be bright, so she proceeded brightly.

'I have been seeing Lord Emsworth off. He's going to London.'

'Yes, he told me. He didn't seem very happy about it.'

'He wasn't,' said Lady Constance, a grim look coming into her face. 'But he must do his duty occasionally as a member of the House of Lords.'

'He'll miss his pig.'

'He can do without her society for a couple of days.'

'And he'll miss his flowers.'

'There are plenty of flowers in London. All he has to do . . . Oh, Heavens!'

'What's the matter?'

'I forgot to tell Clarence to be sure not to pick the flowers in Hyde Park. He will wander off there, and he will pick the flowers. He nearly got arrested once for doing it. Beach!'

'M'lady –?'

'If Lord Emsworth rings up tomorrow and says he is in prison and wants bail, tell him to get in touch immediately with his solicitors. Shoesmith, Shoesmith, Shoesmith and Shoesmith of Lincoln's Inn Fields.'

'Very good, m'lady.'

'I shan't be here.'

'No, m'lady. I quite understand.'

'He's sure to have forgotten their name.'

'I will refresh his lordship's memory.'

'Thank you, Beach.'

'Not at all, m'lady!'

Myra Schoonmaker was staring at her hostess. Her voice trembled a little as she said:

'You won't be here, Lady Constance?'

'I have to go to my hairdresser's in Shrewsbury, and I am lunching with some friends there. I shall be back for dinner, of course. And now I really must be going and finishing that letter to your father. I'll give him your love.'

'Yes, do,' said Myra, and sped off to Lord Emsworth's study, where there was a telephone. The number of the man she loved was graven on her heart. He was staying temporarily with his old Oxford friend, Lord Ickenham's nephew, Pongo Twistleton. But until now there had been no opportunity to call it.

Seated at the instrument with a wary eye on the door, for though Lord Emsworth had left, who knew that Lavender Briggs might not pop in at any moment, she heard the bell ringing in distant London, and presently a voice spoke.

'Darling!' said Myra. 'Is that you, darling? This is me, darling.'

'Darling!' said the voice devoutly.

'Darling,' said Myra, 'the most wonderful thing has happened, darling. Lady Constance is having her hair done tomorrow.'

'Oh, yes?' said the voice, seeming a little puzzled, as if wondering whether it would be in order to express a hope that she would have a fine day for it.

'Don't you get it, dumb-bell? She has to go to Shrewsbury, and she'll be away all day, so I can dash up to London and we can get married.'

There was a momentary silence at the other end of the wire.

One would have gathered that the owner of the voice had had his breath taken away. Recovering it, he said:

'I see.'

'Aren't you pleased?'

'Oh, rather!'

'Well, you don't sound as if you were. Listen, darling. When I was in London, I did a good deal of looking around for registry offices, just in case. I found one in Milton Street. Meet me there tomorrow at two sharp. I must hang up now, darling. Somebody may come in. Good-bye, darling.'

'Good-bye, darling.'

'Till tomorrow, darling.'

'Right ho, darling.'

'Good-bye, darling.'

And if they're listening in at the Market Blandings exchange, thought Myra, as she replaced the receiver, that'll give them something to chat about over their tea and crumpets.

CHAPTER TWO

I

'And now,' said Pongo Twistleton, crushing out his cigarette in the ash tray and speaking with a note of quiet satisfaction in his voice, 'I shall have to be buzzing along. Got a date.'

He had been giving his uncle, Lord Ickenham, lunch at the Drones Club, and a very agreeable function he had found it, for the other, who like Lord Emsworth had graced the opening of Parliament with his presence, had been very entertaining on the subject of his experiences. But what had given him even more pleasure than his relative's mordant critique of the appearance of the four pursuivants, Rouge Croix, Bluemantle, Rouge Dragon and Portcullis, as they headed the procession, had been the stimulating thought that, having this engagement, he ran no risk at the conclusion of the meal of being enticed by his guest into what the latter called one of their pleasant and instructive afternoons. The ordeal of sharing these in the past had never failed to freeze his blood. The occasion when they had gone to the dog races together some years previously remained particularly green in his memory.

Of Frederick Altamont Cornwallis Twistleton, fifth Earl of

Ickenham, a thoughtful critic had once said that in the late afternoon of his life he retained, together with a juvenile waistline, the bright enthusiasms and fresh, unspoiled outlook of a slightly inebriated undergraduate, and no one who knew him would have disputed the accuracy of the statement. As a young man in America, before a number of deaths in the family had led to his succession to the title, he had been at various times a cowboy, a soda-jerker, a newspaper reporter and a prospector in the Mojave Desert, and there was not a ranch, a drug-store, a newspaper office or a sandy waste with which he had been connected that he had not done his best to enliven. His hair today was grey, but it was still his aim to enliven, as far as lay within his power, any environment in which he found himself. He liked, as he often said, to spread sweetness and light or, as he sometimes put it, give service with a smile. He was a tall distinguished-looking man with a jaunty moustache and an alert and enterprising eye. In this eye, as he turned it on his nephew, there was a look of disappointment and reproach, as if he had expected better things from one of his flesh and blood.

'You are leaving me? Why is that? I had been hoping for –'

'I know,' said Pongo austerely. 'One of our pleasant and instructive afternoons. Well, pleasant and instructive afternoons are off. I've got to see a man.'

'About a dog?'

'Not so much about a dog as –'

'Phone him and put him off.'

'I can't.'

'Who is this fellow?'

'Bill Bailey.'

Lord Ickenham seemed surprised.

'He's back, is he?'

'Eh?'

'I was given to understand that he had left home. I seem to remember his wife being rather concerned about it.'

Pongo saw that his uncle had got everything mixed up, as elderly gentlemen will.

'Oh, this chap isn't really Bill. I believe he was christened Cuthbert. But if a fellow's name is Bailey, you've more or less got to call him Bill.'

'Of course, noblesse oblige. Friend of yours?'

'Bosom. Up at Oxford with him.'

'Tell him to join us here.'

'Can't be done. I've arranged to meet him in Milton Street.'

'Where's that?'

'In South Kensington.'

Lord Ickenham pursed his lips.

'South Kensington? Where sin stalks naked through the dark alleys and only might is right. Give this man a miss. He'll lead you astray.'

'He won't jolly well lead me astray. And why? Because for one thing he's a curate and for another he's getting married. The rendezvous is at the Milton Street registry office.'

'You are his witness?'

'That's right.'

'And who is the bride?'

'American girl.'

'Nice?'

'Bill speaks well of her.'

'What's her name?'

'Schoonmaker.'

Lord Ickenham leaped in his seat.

'Good heavens! Not little Myra Schoonmaker?'

'I don't know if she's little or not. I've never seen her. But her name's Myra all right. Why – do you know her?'

A tender look had come into Lord Ickenham's handsome face. He twirled his moustache sentimentally.

'Do I know her! Many's the time I've given her her bath. Not recently, of course, but years ago when I was earning my living in New York. Jimmy Schoonmaker was my great buddy in those days. I don't get over to God's country much now, your aunt thinks it better otherwise, and I've often wondered how he was making out. He promised, when I knew him, to become a big shot in the financial world. Even then, though comparatively young, he was able to shoot a cigar across his face without touching it with his fingers, which we all know is the first step to establishing oneself as a tycoon. I expect by this time he's the Wolf of Wall Street, and is probably offended if he isn't investigated every other week by a Senate commission. Well, it all seems very odd to me.'

'What's odd?'

'His daughter getting married at a registry office. I should have thought she would have had a big choral wedding with bridesmaids and bishops and all the fixings.'

'Ah, I see what you mean.' Pongo looked cautiously over his shoulder. No one appeared to be within earshot. 'Yes, you would think so, wouldn't you? But Bill's nuptials have got to be solemnized with more than a spot of secrecy and silence. The course of true love hasn't been running too smooth. Hell-hounds have been bunging spanners into it.'

'What hell-hounds would those be?'

'I should have said one hell-hound. You know her. Lady Constance Keeble.'

'What, dear old Connie? How that name brings back fragrant memories. I wonder if you recall the time when you and I went to Blandings Castle, I posing as Sir Roderick Glossop, the loony doctor, you as his nephew Basil?'

'I recall it,' said Pongo with a strong shudder. The visit alluded to had given him nightmares for months.

'Happy days, happy days! I enjoyed my stay enormously, and wish I could repeat it. The bracing air, the pleasant society, the occasional refreshing look at Emsworth's pig, it all combined to pep me up and brush away the cobwebs. But how does Connie come into it?'

'She forbade the banns.'

'I still don't follow the scenario. Why was she in a position to do so?'

'What happened was this. She and Schoonmaker are old pals – I got all this from Bill, so I assume we can take it as accurate – and he wanted his daughter to have a London season, so he brought her over here and left her in Lady C.'s charge.'

'All clear so far.'

'And plumb spang in the middle of their London season Lady C. discovered that the beazel was walking out with Bill. Ascertaining that he was a curate, she became as sore as a gumboil.'

'She does not like curates?'

'That's the idea one gets.'

'Odd. She doesn't like me, either. Very hard to please, that woman. What's wrong with curates?'

'Well, they're all pretty hard up. Bill hasn't a bean.'

'I begin to see. Humble suitor. Curious how prejudiced so many people are against humble suitors. My own case is one in point. When I was courting your Aunt Jane, her parents took the bleakest view of the situation, and weren't their faces red when one day I suddenly became that noblest of created beings, an Earl, a hell of a fellow with four christian names and a coronet hanging on a peg in the downstairs cupboard. Her father, scorning me because I was a soda-jerker at the time, frequently, I believe, alluded to me as "that bum", but it was very different when I presented myself at his Park Avenue residence with a coronet on the back of my head and a volume of Debrett under my arm. He gave me his blessing and a cigar. No chance of Bill Bailey becoming an earl, I suppose?'

'Not unless he murders about fifty-seven uncles and cousins.'

'Which a curate, of course, would hesitate to do. So what was Connie's procedure?'

'She lugged the poor wench off to Blandings, and she's been there ever since, practically in durance vile, her every movement watched. But this Myra seems to be a sensible, level-headed girl, because, learning from her spies that Lady C. was to go to Shrewsbury for a hair-do and wouldn't be around till dinner time, she phoned Bill that she would be free that day and would nip up to London and marry him. She told him to meet her at the Milton Street registry office, where the project could be put through speedily and at small expense.'

'I see. Very shrewd. I often think these runaway marriages are best. No fuss and feathers. After all, who wants a lot of bishops cluttering up the place? I often say, when you've seen one bishop, you've seen them all.' Lord Ickenham paused. 'Well,' he said, looking at his watch. 'I suppose it's about time we were getting along. Don't want to be late.'

Pongo started. To his sensitive ears this sounded extremely

like the beginning of one of their pleasant and instructive afternoons. In just such a tone of voice had his relative a few years earlier suggested that they might look in at the dog races, for there was, he said, no better way of studying the soul of the people than to mingle with them in their simple pastimes.

'We? You aren't coming?'

'Of course I'm coming. Two witnesses are always better than one, and little Myra –'

'I can't guarantee that she's little.'

'And Myra, whatever her size, would never forgive me if I were not there to hold her hand when the firing squad assembles.'

Pongo chewed his lower lip, this way and that dividing the swift mind.

'Well, all right. But no larks.'

'My dear boy! As if I should dream of being frivolous on such a sacred occasion. Of course, if I find this Bill Bailey of yours unworthy of her, I shall put a stopper on the proceedings, as any man of sensibility would. What sort of chap is he? Pale and fragile, I suppose, with a touch of consumption and a tendency to recite the collect for the day in a high tenor voice?'

'Pale and fragile, my foot. He boxed three years for Oxford.'

'He did?'

'And went through the opposition like a dose of salts.'

'Then all should be well. I expect I shall take the fellow to my bosom.'

His expectation was fulfilled. The Rev Cuthbert Bailey met with his instant approval. He liked his curates substantial, and Bill proved to be definitely the large economy size, the sort of curate whom one could picture giving the local backslider the choice between seeing the light or getting plugged in the eye. Amplifying his earlier remarks, Pongo on the journey to Milton Street had told his uncle that in the parish of Bottleton East, where he had recently held a cure of souls, Bill Bailey had been universally respected, and Lord Ickenham could readily appreciate why. He himself would have treated with the utmost respect any young man so obviously capable of a sweet left hook followed by a snappy right to the button. A captious critic might have felt on seeing the Rev Cuthbert that it would have been more suitable for one in holy orders to have looked a little less like the logical contender for the world's heavyweight championship, but it was impossible to regard his rugged features and bulging shoulders without an immediate feeling of awe. Impossible, too, not to like his manifest honesty and simplicity. It seemed to Lord Ickenham that in probing beneath the forbidding exterior to the gentle soul it hid his little Myra had done the smart thing.

They fell into pleasant conversation, but after the first few exchanges it was plain to Lord Ickenham that the young man of God was becoming extremely nervous. Nor was the reason for this difficult to divine. Some twenty minutes had elapsed, and there were still no signs of the bride-to-be, and nothing so surely saps the morale of a bridegroom on his wedding day as the failure of the party of the second part to put in an appearance at the tryst.

Ten minutes later, Bill Bailey rose, his homely features registering anguish.

'She isn't coming?'

Lord Ickenham tried to comfort him with the quite erroneous statement that it was early yet. Pongo, also anxious to be helpful, said he would go out and cock an eye up and down the street to see if there were any signs of her. His departure from the room synchronized with a hollow groan from the suffering young man.

'I must have put her off!'

Lord Ickenham raised a sympathetic but puzzled eyebrow.

'I don't think I understand you. Put her off? How?'

'By the way I spoke on the phone. You see, I was a bit doubtful of this idea of hers. It didn't seem right somehow that she should be taking this terrifically important step without thinking it over. I mean, I've so little to offer her. I thought we ought to wait till I get a vicarage.'

'I follow you now. You had scruples?'

'Yes.'

'Did you tell her so?'

'No, but she must have noticed something odd in my voice, because she asked me if I wasn't pleased.'

'To which you replied –?'

'"Oh, rather!"'

Lord Ickenham shook his head.

'You should have done better than that. Or did you say "Oh, ra-a-a-ther!", emphasizing it and dragging it out, as it were? Joyously, if you know what I mean, with a sort of lilt in the voice?'

'I'm afraid I didn't. You see –'

'I know. You had scruples. That's the curate in you coming out. You must fight against this tendency. You don't suppose Young Lochinvar had scruples, do you? You know the poem about Young Lochinvar?'

'Oh, yes. I used to recite it as a kid.'

'I, too, and to solid applause, though there were critics who considered that I was better at "It wath the schcooner

Hesperuth that thailed the thtormy thea". I was rather short on front teeth in those days. But despite these scruples you came to this marriage depot.'

'Yes.'

'And the impression you have given me is that your one desire is to have the registrar start doing his stuff.'

'Yes.'

'You overcame your scruples?'

'Yes.'

'I quite understand. I've done the same thing myself. I suppose if the scruples I've overcome in my time were laid end to end, they would reach from London to Glasgow. Ah, Pongo,' said Lord Ickenham, as his nephew appeared in the doorway. 'Anything to report?'

'Not a thing. Not a single female as far as the eye could reach. I'll tell you what occurred to me, Bill, as I was scanning the horizon.'

'Probably the very thing that has just occurred to me,' said Lord Ickenham. 'You were thinking that Lady Constance must have changed her mind about going to Shrewsbury for that hair-do.'

'That's right. And with her on the premises, the popsy –'

Bill's rugged features registered displeasure.

'I wish you wouldn't call her a popsy.'

'With her on the premises, your ball of worsted would naturally be unable to make her getaway. You'll probably receive a letter tomorrow explaining the situation and making arrangements for the next fixture.'

'Yes, that must be it,' said Bill, brightening a little. 'Though you'd have thought she would have wired,' he added, sinking into the depths again.

Lord Ickenham patted his burly shoulder paternally.

'My dear chap! How could she? The Market Blandings post office is two miles from the castle and, as Pongo says, her every movement is watched. She'll be lucky if she gets so much as a letter through the lines without having it steamed open and intercepted. If I were you, I wouldn't worry for a moment.'

'I'll try not to,' said Bill, heaving a sigh that shook the room. 'Well, anyway, there's no sense in hanging around here. This place gives me the creeps. Thanks for coming along, Pongo. Thanks for coming along, Lord Ickenham. Sorry your time was wasted.'

'My dear fellow, time is never wasted when it is passed in pleasant company.'

'No. No. There's that, of course. Well, I'll be off.'

As the door closed behind him, Lord Ickenham sighed, not so vigorously as Bill had done but with a wealth of compassion. He mourned in spirit for the young cleric.

'Too bad,' he said. 'It is always difficult for a bridegroom to key himself up to going through the wedding ceremony, an ordeal that taxes the stoutest, and when he's done it and the bride doesn't meet him half way, the iron enters into the soul pretty deeply. And no knowing when the vigilance of the authorities will be relaxed again, I suppose, if ever. You don't make prison breaks easily when Connie is holding the jailer's keys.'

Pongo nodded. He, too, mourned in spirit for his stricken friend.

'No,' he said. 'I'm afraid Bill's in a spot. And what makes the situation stickier is that Archie Gilpin's at Blandings.'

'Who?'

'The Duke of Dunstable's nephew.'

'Ricky Gilpin's brother?'

'That's right. You ever met him?'

'Never. I know Dunstable, of course, and I know Ricky, but this Archibald is a sealed book to me. Who told you he was at Blandings?'

'He did. In person. I ran into him yesterday and he said he was off there on the afternoon train. Pretty sinister, it seemed to me.'

'Why is that?'

'Well, dash it, there he'll be closeted with the girl, and who knows she won't decide to switch from Bill to him? He's a very good-looking bloke. Which you can't say Bill is.'

'No, I would call Bill's an interesting rather than a beautiful face. He reminds me a little of one of my colleagues on the Wyoming ranch where I held a salaried position in my younger days as a cow-puncher, of whom another of my colleagues, a gifted phrasemaker, said that he had a face that would stop a clock. No doubt Bill has stopped dozens. But surely the little Myra I used to wrap in a bath towel and dandle on my knee can't have grown up into the sort of girl who attaches all that importance to looks.'

'You never know. Girls do go for the finely-chiselled. And apart from his looks, he's an artist, and there's something about artists that seems to act on the other sex like catnip on cats. What's more, I happen to know, because I met a fellow who knows a chap who knows her, that Archie's girl has just broken their engagement.'

'Indeed?'

'A girl called Millicent Rigby. Archie works on one of those papers Lord Tilbury runs at the Mammoth Publishing Company, and she's Tilbury's secretary. This fellow told me that the chap had told him that he had had it direct from the Rigby wench that she had handed Archie the black spot. You see what that means?'

'Not altogether.'

'Use your bean, Uncle Fred. You know what you do when your girl gives you the push. You dash off and propose to another girl, just to show her she isn't the only onion in the stew.'

Lord Ickenham nodded. It was many years since he had acted in the manner described, but he, too, had lived in Arcady.

'Ah, youth, youth!' he was saying to himself, and he shuddered a little as he recalled the fearful female down Greenwich Village way, all beads and bangles and matted hair, at whose sandalled feet he had laid his heart the second time Pongo's Aunt Jane had severed relations with him.

'Yes, I follow you now. This does make Archibald a menace, and one cannot but feel a certain anxiety for Bill. Where can I find him, by the way?'

'He's staying with me at my flat. Why?'

'I was thinking I might look in on him from time to time and try to cheer him up. Take him to the dog races, perhaps.'

Pongo quivered like an aspen. He always quivered like an aspen when reminded of the afternoon when he had attended the dog races in Lord Ickenham's company. Though on that occasion, as his uncle had often pointed out, a wiser policeman would have been content with a mere reprimand.

2

The canny peer of the realm, when duty calls him to lend his presence to the ceremony of the Opening of Parliament, hires his robes and coronet from that indispensable clothing firm, the Brothers Moss of Covent Garden, whose boast is that they can at any time fit anyone out as anything and have him ready to go anywhere. Only they can prevent him being caught short. It was to their emporium that, after leaving his nephew, Lord Ickenham repaired, carrying a suitcase. And he had returned the suitcase's contents and paid his modest bill, when there entered, also carrying a suitcase, a tall, limp, drooping figure, at the sight of which he uttered a glad cry.

'Emsworth! My dear fellow, how nice to run into you again. So you too are bringing back your sheaves?'

'Eh?' said Lord Emsworth, who always said 'Eh?' when anyone addressed him suddenly. 'Oh, hullo, Ickenham. Are you in London?'

Lord Ickenham assured him that he was, and Lord Emsworth said so was he. This having been straightened out,

'Were you at that thing this morning?' he said.

'I was indeed,' said Lord Ickenham, 'and looking magnificent. I don't suppose there is a peer in England who presents a posher appearance when wearing the reach-me-downs and comic hat than I do. Just before the procession got under way, I heard Rouge Croix whisper to Bluemantle "Don't look now, but who's that chap over there?", and Bluemantle whispered back, "I haven't the foggiest, but evidently some terrific swell." But it's nice to get out of the fancy dress, isn't it, and it's wonderful seeing you, Emsworth. How's the Empress?'

'Eh? Oh, capital, capital, capital. I left her in the care of my pigman Wellbeloved, in whom I have every confidence.'

'Splendid. Well, let's go and have a couple for the tonsils and a pleasant chat. I know a little bar round the corner,' said Lord Ickenham, who, wherever he was, always knew a little bar round the corner. 'You have rather a fatigued air, as if putting on all that dog this morning had exhausted you. A whisky with a splash of soda will soon bring back the sparkle to your eyes.'

Seated in the little bar round the corner, Lord Ickenham regarded his companion with some concern.

'Yes,' he said. 'I was right. You don't look your usual bonny self. Very testing, these Openings of Parliament. Usually I give them a miss, as no doubt you do. What brought you up today?'

'Connie insisted.'

'I understand. There are, I should imagine, few finer right-and-left-hand insisters than Lady Constance. Charming woman, of course.'

'Connie?' said Lord Emsworth, surprised.

'Though perhaps not everybody's cup of tea,' said Lord Ickenham, sensing the incredulity in his companion's voice. 'But tell me, how is everything at Blandings Castle? Jogging along nicely, I hope. I always look on that little shack of yours as an earthly Paradise.'

It was not within Lord Emsworth's power to laugh bitterly, but he uttered a bleating sound which was as near as he could get to a bitter laugh. The description of Blandings Castle as an earthly Paradise, with his sister Constance, the Duke, Lavender Briggs, and the Church Lads' Brigade running around loose there, struck him as ironical. He mused for a space in silence.

'I don't know what to do, Ickenham,' he said, his sombre train of thought coming to its terminus.

'You mean now? Have another.'

'No, no, thank you, really. It is very unusual for me to indulge in alcoholic stimulant so early in the day. I was referring to conditions at Blandings Castle.'

'Not so good?'

'They are appalling. I have a new secretary, the worst I have ever had. Worse than Baxter.'

'That seems scarcely credible.'

'I assure you. A girl of the name of Briggs. She persecutes me.'

'Get rid of her.'

'How can I? Connie engaged her. And the Duke of Dunstable is staying at the castle.'

'What, again?'

'And the Church Lads' Brigade are camping in the park, yelling and squealing all the time, and I am convinced that it was one of them who threw a roll at my top hat.'

'Your top hat? When did you ever wear a top hat?'

'It was at the school treat. Connie always makes me wear a top hat at the school treat. I went into the tent at teatime to see that everything was going along all right, and as I was passing down the aisle between the tables, a boy threw a crusty roll at my hat and knocked it off. Nothing will persuade me, Ickenham, that the culprit was not one of the Church Lads.'

'But you have no evidence that would stand up in a court of law?'

'Eh? No, none.'

'Too bad. Well, the whole set-up sounds extraordinarily like Devil's Island, and I am not surprised that you find it difficult to keep the upper lip as stiff as one likes to see upper lips.' A strange light had come into Lord Ickenham's eyes. His nephew Pongo would have recognized it. It was the light which had so often come into them when the other was suggesting that they embark on one of their pleasant and instructive afternoons. 'What you need, it seems to me,' he said, 'is some rugged ally at your side, someone who will quell the secretary, look Connie in the eye and make her wilt, take the Duke off your hands and generally spread sweetness and light.'

'Ah!' said Lord Emsworth with a sigh, as he allowed his mind to dwell on this utopian picture.

'Would you like me to come to Blandings?'

Lord Emsworth started. His pince-nez, which always dropped off his nose when he was deeply stirred, did an adagio dance at the end of their string.

'Would you?'

'Nothing would please me more. When do you return there?'

'Tomorrow. This is very good of you, Ickenham.'

'Not at all. We earls must stick together. There is just one thing. You won't mind if I bring a friend with me? I would not ask you, but he's just back from Brazil and would be rather lost in London without me.'

'Brazil? Do people live in Brazil!'

'Frequently, I believe. This chap has been there some years. He is connected with the Brazil nut industry. I am a little sketchy as to what his actual job is, but I think he's the fellow who squeezes the nuts in the squeezer, to give them that peculiar shape. I may be wrong, of course. Then I bring him with me?'

'Certainly, certainly, certainly. Delighted, delighted.'

'A wise decision on your part. Who knows that he may not help the general composition? He might fall in love with the secretary and marry her and take her to Brazil.'

'True.'

'Or murder the Duke with some little-known Asiatic poison. Or be of assistance in a number of other ways. I'm sure you'll be glad to have him about the place. He is house-broken and eats whatever you're having yourself. What train are you taking tomorrow?'

'The 11.45 from Paddington.'

'Expect us there, my dear Emsworth,' said Lord Ickenham. 'And not only there, but with our hair in a braid and, speaking for myself, prepared to be up and doing with a heart for any fate. I'll go and ring my friend up now and tell him to start packing.'

3

It was some hours later that Pongo Twistleton, having a tissue-restorer before dinner in the Drones Club smoking-room, was informed by the smoking-room waiter that a gentleman was in the hall, asking to see him, and a shadow fell on his tranquil mood. Too often when gentlemen called asking to see members of the Drones Club, their visits had to do with accounts rendered for goods supplied, with the subject of remittances which would oblige cropping up, and he knew that his own affairs were in a state of some disorder.

'Is he short and stout?' he asked nervously, remembering that the representative of the Messrs Hicks and Adrian, to whom he owed a princely sum for shirting, socks and under-linen could be so described.

'Far from it. Tall and beautifully slender,' said a hearty voice behind him. 'Svelte may be the word I am groping for.'

'Oh, hullo, Uncle Fred,' said Pongo, relieved. 'I thought you were someone else.'

'Rest assured that I am not. First, last and all the time yours to command Ickenham! I took the liberty of walking in, my dear Pongo, confident that I would receive a nephew's welcome. We Ickenhams dislike to wait in halls. It offends our pride. What's that you're having? Order me one of the same. I suppose it will harden my arteries but I like them hard. Bill not with you tonight?'

'No. He had to go to Bottleton East to pick up some things.'

'You have not seen him recently?'

'No, I haven't been back to the flat. Do you want me to give you dinner?'

'Just what I was about to suggest. It will be your last opportunity for some little time. I'm off to Blandings Castle tomorrow.'

'You're . . . *what*?'

'Yes, after I left you I ran into Emsworth and he asked me to drop down there for a few days or possibly longer. He's having trouble, poor chap.'

'What's wrong with him?'

'Practically everything. He has a new secretary who harries him. The Duke of Dunstable seems to be a fixture on the premises. Lady Constance has pinched his favourite hat and given it to the deserving poor, and he lives in constant fear of her getting away with his shooting jacket with the holes in the elbows. In addition to which, he is much beset by Church Lads.'

'Eh?'

'You see how full my hands will be, if I am to help him. I shall have to devise some means of ridding him of this turbulent secretary –'

'Church Lads?'

' – shipping the Duke back to Wiltshire, where he belongs, curbing Connie and putting the fear of God into these Church Lads. An impressive programme, and one that would be beyond the scope of a lesser man. Most fortunately I am not a lesser man.'

'How do you mean, Church Lads?'

'Weren't you ever a Church Lad?'

'No.'

'Well, many of the younger generation are: They assemble in gangs in most rural parishes. The Church Lads' Brigade they call themselves. Connie has allowed them to camp out by the lake.'

'And Emsworth doesn't like them?'

'Nobody could, except their mothers. No, he eyes them askance. They ruin the scenery, poison the air with their uncouth cries, and at the recent school treat, so he tells me, knocked off his top hat with a crusty roll.'

Pongo shook his head censoriously.

'He shouldn't have worn a topper at a school treat,' he said. He was remembering functions of this kind into which he had been lured at one time and another by clergymen's daughters for whose charms he had fallen. The one at Maiden Eggesford in Somerset, when his great love for Angelica Briscoe, daughter of the Rev P. P. Briscoe, who vetted the souls of the peasantry in that hamlet, had led him to put his head in a sack and allow himself to be prodded with sticks by the younger set, had never been erased from his memory. 'A topper! Good Lord! Just asking for it!'

'He acted under duress. He would have preferred to wear a cloth cap, but Connie insisted. You know how persuasive she can be.'

'She's a tough baby.'

'Very tough. Let us hope she takes to Bill Bailey.'

'Does what?'

'Oh, I didn't tell you, did I? Bill is accompanying me to Blandings.'

'What!'

'Yes, Emsworth very kindly included him in his invitation. We're off tomorrow on the 11.45, singing a gypsy song.'

Horror leaped into Pongo's eyes. He started violently, and came within an ace of spilling his martini with a spot of lemon peel in it. Fond though he was of his Uncle Fred, he had never wavered in his view that in the interests of young English manhood he ought to be kept on a chain and seldom allowed at large.

'But my gosh!'

'Something's troubling you?'

'You can't . . . what's the word . . . you can't subject poor old Bill to this frightful ordeal.'

Lord Ickenham's eyebrows rose.

'Well, really, Pongo, if you consider it an ordeal for a young man to be in the same house with the girl he loves, you must have less sentiment in you than I had supposed.'

'Yes, that's all very well. His ball of fluff will be there, I agree. But what good's that going to do him when two minutes after his arrival Lady Constance grabs him by the seat of the trousers and heaves him out?'

'I anticipate no such contingency. You seem to have a very odd idea of the sort of thing that goes on at Blandings Castle, my boy. You appear to look on that refined home as a kind of Bowery saloon with bodies being hurled through the swing doors all the time, and bounced along the sidewalk. Nothing of that nature will occur. We shall be like a great big family. Peace and good will everywhere. Too bad you won't be with us.'

'I'm all right here, thanks,' said Pongo with a slight shudder as he recalled some of the high spots of his previous visit to the castle. 'But I still maintain that when Lady Constance hears the name Bailey –'

'But she won't. You don't suppose a shrewd man like myself would have overlooked a point like that. He's calling himself Cuthbert Meriwether. I told him to write it down and memorize it.'

'She'll find out.'

'Not a chance. Who's going to tell her?'

Pongo gave up the struggle. He knew the futility of arguing, and he had just perceived the bright side to the situation – to wit, that after tomorrow more than a hundred miles would separate him from his amiable but hair-bleaching relative. The thought was a very heartening one. Going by the form book, he took it for granted that ere many suns had set the old buster would be up to some kind of hell which would ultimately stagger civilization and turn the moon to blood, but what mattered was that he would be up to it at Lord Emsworth's rural seat and not in London. How right, he felt, the author of the well-known hymn had been in saying that peace, perfect peace is to be attained only when loved ones are far away.

'Let's go in and have some dinner,' he said.

CHAPTER THREE

I

One of the things that made Lord Emsworth such a fascinating travelling companion was the fact that shortly after the start of any journey he always fell into a restful sleep. The train bearing him and guests to Market Blandings had glided from the platform of Paddington station, as promised by the railway authorities, whose word is their bond, at 11.45, and at 12.10 he was lying back in his seat with his eyes closed, making little whistling noises punctuated at intervals by an occasional snort. Lord Ickenham, accordingly, was able to talk to the junior member of the party without risk, always to be avoided when there is plotting afoot, of being overheard.

'Nervous, Bill?' he said, regarding the Rev Cuthbert sympathetically. He had seemed to notice during the early stages of the journey a tendency on the other's part to twitch like a galvanized frog and allow a sort of glaze to creep over his eyes.

Bill Bailey breathed deeply.

'I'm feeling as I did when I tottered up the pulpit steps to deliver my first sermon.'

'I quite understand. While there is no more admirably

educational experience for a young fellow starting out in life than going to stay at a country house under a false name, it does tend to chill the feet to no little extent. Pongo, though he comes from a stout-hearted family, felt just as you do when I took him to Blandings Castle as Sir Roderick Glossop's nephew Basil. I remember telling him at the time that he reminded me of Hamlet. The same moodiness and irresolution, coupled with a strongly marked disposition to get out of the train and walk back to London. Having become accustomed to this kind of thing myself, so much so that now I don't think it quite sporting to go to stay with people under my own name, I have lost the cat-on-hot-bricks feeling which I must have had at one time, but I can readily imagine that for a novice an experience of this sort cannot fail to be quite testing. Your sermon was a success, I trust?'

'Well, they didn't rush the pulpit.'

'You are too modest, Bill Bailey. I'll bet you had them rolling in the aisles and carried out on stretchers. And this visit to Blandings Castle will, I know, prove equally triumphant. You are probably asking yourself what I am hoping to accomplish by it. Nothing actually constructive, but I think it essential for you to keep an eye on this Archibald Gilpin of whom I have heard so much. Pongo tells me he is an artist, and you know how dangerous they are. Watch him closely. Every time he suggests to Myra an after-dinner stroll to the lake to look at the moonlight glimmering on the water – and on the Church Lads' Brigade too, of course, for I understand that they are camping out down there – you must join the hikers.'

'Yes.'

'That's the spirit. And the same thing applies to any attempt on his part to get the . . . popsy is the term you use, is it not?'

'It is not the term I use. It's the term Pongo uses, and I've had to speak to him about it.'

'I'm sorry. Any attempt on his part, I should have said, to get the girl you love into the rose garden must be countered with the same firmness and resolution. But I can leave that to you. Tell me, how did you two happen to meet?'

A rugged face like Bill Bailey's could never really be a mirror of the softer emotions, but something resembling a tender look did come into it. If their host had not at this moment uttered a sudden snort rather like that of Empress of Blandings on beholding linseed meal, Lord Ickenham would have heard him sigh sentimentally.

'You remember that song, the Limehouse Blues?'

'It is one I frequently sing in my bath. But aren't we changing the subject?'

'No, what I was going to say was that she had heard the song over in America, and she'd read that book *Limehouse Nights*, and she was curious to see the place. So she sneaked off one afternoon and went there. Well, Limehouse is next door to Bottleton East, where my job was, and I happened to be doing some visiting there for a pal of mine who had sprained an ankle while trying to teach the choir boys to dance the carioca, and I came along just as someone was snatching her bag. So, of course, I biffed the blighter.'

'Where did they bury the unfortunate man?'

'Oh, I didn't biff him much, just enough to make him see how wrong it is to snatch bags.'

'And then?'

'Well, one thing led to another, sort of.'

'I see. And what is she like these days?'

'You know her?'

'In her childhood we were quite intimate. She used to call me Uncle Fred. Extraordinarily pretty she was then. Still is, I hope?'

'Yes.'

'That's good. So many attractive children lose their grip and go all to pieces in later life.'

'Yes.'

'But she didn't?'

'No.'

'Still comely, is she?'

'Yes.'

'And you would die for one little rose from her hair?'

'Yes.'

'There is no peril, such for instance as having Lady Constance Keeble look squiggle-eyed at you, that you would not face for her sake?'

'No.'

'Your conversational method, my dear Bill,' said Lord Ickenham, regarding him approvingly, 'impresses me a good deal and has shown me that I must change the set-up as I had envisaged it. I had planned on arrival at the castle to draw you out on the subject of Brazil, so that you could hold everybody spellbound with your fund of good stories about your adventures there and make yourself the life of the party, but I feel now that that is not the right approach.'

'Brazil?'

'Ah, yes, I didn't mention that to you, did I? I told Emsworth that there was where you came from.'

'Why Brazil?'

'Oh, one gets these ideas. But I was saying that I had changed my mind about featuring you as a sparkling raconteur.

Having had the pleasure of conversing with you, I see you now as the strong, silent man, the fellow with the far-away look in his eyes who rarely speaks except in monosyllables. So if anybody tries to pump you about Brazil, just grunt. Like our host,' said Lord Ickenham, indicating Lord Emsworth, who was doing so. 'A pity in a way of course, for I had a couple of good stories about the Brazilian ants which would have gone down well. As I dare say you know, they go about eating everything in sight, like Empress of Blandings.'

The sound of that honoured name must have penetrated Lord Emsworth's slumbers, for his eyes opened and he sat up, blinking.

'Did I hear you say something about the Empress?'

'I was telling Meriwether here what a superb animal she was, the only pig that has ever won the silver medal in the Fat Pigs class three years in succession at the Shropshire Agricultural Show. Wasn't I, Meriwether?'

'Yes.'

'He says Yes. You must show her to him first thing.'

'Eh? Oh, of course. Yes, certainly, certainly, certainly,' said Lord Emsworth, well pleased. 'You'll join us, Ickenham?'

'Not immediately, if you don't mind. I yield to no one in my appreciation of the Empress, but I feel that on arrival at the old shanty what I shall need first is a refreshing cup of tea.'

'Tea?' said Lord Emsworth, as if puzzled by the word. 'Tea? Oh, tea? Yes, of course, tea. Don't take it myself, but Connie has it on the terrace every afternoon. She'll look after you.'

2

Lady Constance was alone at the tea-table when Lord Ickenham reached it. As he approached, she lowered the cucumber sandwich with which she had been about to refresh herself and contrived what might have passed for a welcoming smile. To say that she was glad to see Lord Ickenham would be overstating the case, and she had already spoken her mind to her brother Clarence with reference to his imbecility in inviting him – with a friend – to Blandings Castle. But, as she had so often had to remind herself when coping with the Duke of Dunstable, she was a hostess, and a hostess must conceal her emotions.

'So nice to see you again, Lord Ickenham. So glad you were able to come,' she said, not actually speaking from between clenched teeth, but far from warmly. 'Will you have some tea, or would you rather . . . Are you looking for something?'

'Nothing important,' said Lord Ickenham, whose eyes had been flitting to and fro as if he felt something to be missing. 'I had been expecting to see my little friend, Myra Schoonmaker. Doesn't she take her dish of tea of an afternoon?'

'Myra went for a walk. You know her?'

'In her childhood we were quite intimate. Her father was a great friend of mine.'

The rather marked frostiness of Lady Constance's manner melted somewhat. Nothing would ever make her forget what this man in a single brief visit had done to the cloistral peace of Blandings Castle while spreading sweetness and light there, but to a friend of James Schoonmaker much had to be forgiven. In a voice that was almost cordial she said:

'Have you seen him lately?'

'Alas, not for many years. He has this unfortunate habit so many Americans have of living in America.'

Lady Constance sighed. She, too, had deplored this whim of James Schoonmaker's.

'And as my dear wife feels rightly or wrongly that it is safer for me not to be exposed to the temptations of New York but to live a quiet rural life at Ickenham Halls, Hants, our paths have parted, much to my regret. I knew him when he was a junior member of one of those Wall Street firms. I suppose he's a monarch of finance now, rolling in the stuff?'

'He has been very successful, yes.'

'I always predicted that he would be. I never actually saw him talking into three telephones at the same time, for he had not yet reached those heights, but it was obvious that the day would come when he would be able to do it without difficulty.'

'He was over here not long ago. He left Myra with me. He wanted her to have a London season.'

'Just the kindly sort of thing he would do. Did she enjoy it?'

Lady Constance frowned.

'I was unfortunately obliged to take her away from London after we had been there a few weeks. I found that she had become involved with a quite impossible young man.'

There was a shocked horror in Lord Ickenham's 'Tut-tut!'

'She insisted that they were engaged. Absurd, of course.'

'Why absurd?'

'He is a curate.'

'I have known some quite respectable curates.'

'Have you ever known one who had any money?'

'Well, no. They don't often have much, do they? I suppose a curate who was quick with his fingers would make a certain amount out of the Sunday offertory bag, but nothing more than a small, steady income. Did Myra blow her top?'

'I beg your pardon?'

'Is she emotionally disturbed at being parted from the man of her choice?'

'She seems depressed.'

'What she needs is young society. How extremely fortunate that I was able to bring my friend Meriwether with me.'

Lady Constance started. She had momentarily forgotten his friend Meriwether.

'Emsworth took him off to look at the Empress, feeling that it would have a tonic effect after the long railway journey. You'll like Meriwether.'

'Indeed?' said Lady Constance, who considered this point a very moot one. She was strongly of the opinion that any associate of Frederick, fifth Earl of Ickenham, would be as unfit for human consumption as that blot on the peerage himself. The slight flicker of friendliness resulting from the discovery that he had at one time been on cordial terms with the man who meant so much to her had died away, and only the memory of his last visit to the castle remained. She wished she did not remember that visit so clearly. Like quite a number of those whose paths Lord Ickenham had crossed, she wanted to forget the past. Pongo Twistleton would have understood how she felt.

'You have known Mr Meriwether a long time?' she said.

'From boyhood. His boyhood, of course, not mine.'

'He comes from Brazil, I hear.'

'Yes, like Charley's Aunt. But –' Here Lord Ickenham's voice took on a grave note, '– on no account mention Brazil to him if you don't mind. It was the scene of the great tragedy of his life. His young wife fell into the Amazon and was eaten by an alligator.'

'How dreadful!'

'For her, yes, though not of course for the alligator. I thought I had better give you this word of warning. Pass it along, will you? Oh, hullo, Dunstable.'

The Duke had lumbered on to the terrace and was peering at him in his popeyed way.

'Hullo, Ickenham. You here again?'

'That's right.'

'You've aged.'

'Not spiritually. My heart is still the heart of a little child.'

'Pass what along?'

'Ah, you overheard what I was saying? I was speaking of my friend Meriwether, whom Lady Constance very kindly invited here with me.'

It would be too much, perhaps, to say that Lady Constance snorted at this explanation of Bill's presence in the home, but she unquestionably sniffed. She said nothing, and ate a cucumber sandwich in rather a marked manner. She was thinking that she would have more to say to her brother Clarence on this subject when she got him alone.

'What about him?'

'I was urging Lady Constance not to speak to him of Brazil. Will you remember this?'

'What would I want to speak to him of Brazil for?'

'You might on learning that that was where he had spent much of his life. And if you did, a far-away look would come into his eyes and he would grunt with pain. His young wife fell into the Amazon.'

'Potty thing to do.'

'And was eaten by an alligator.'

'Well, what else did the silly ass expect would happen? Connie,' said the Duke, dismissing a topic that had failed from the start to grip him. 'Stop stuffing yourself with food and come along. Young George wants to take some pictures of us with his camera. He's out on the lawn with Archibald. You met my nephew, Archibald?'

'Not yet,' said Lord Ickenham. 'I am looking forward eagerly to making his acquaintance.'

'You're *what*?' said the Duke incredulously.

'Any nephew of yours.'

'Oh I see what you mean. But you can't go by that. He's not like me. He's potty.'

'Indeed?'

'Got less brain than Connie here, and hasn't the excuse for pottiness that she has, because he's not a woman. Connie's hoping he'll marry the Stick-in-the-Mud girl, though why any girl would want to tie herself up with a poop like that, is more than I can imagine. He's an artist. Draws pictures. And you know what artists are. Where is the Tiddlypush girl, Connie? George wants her in the picture.'

'She went down to the lake.'

'Well, if she thinks I'm going there to fetch her, she's mistaken,' said the Duke gallantly. 'George'll have to do without her.'

3

On a knoll overlooking the lake there stood a little sort of imitation Greek temple, erected by Lord Emsworth's grandfather in the days when landowners went in for little sort of imitation Greek temples in their grounds. In front of it there was a marble bench, and on this bench Myra Schoonmaker was sitting, gazing with what are called unseeing eyes at the Church Lads bobbing about in the water below. She was not in the gayest of spirits. Her brow, indeed, was as furrowed and her lips as drawn as they had been three days earlier when she had accompanied Lord Emsworth to the Empress's sty.

A footstep on the marble floor brought her out of her reverie with a jerk. She turned and saw a tall, distinguished-looking man with grey hair and a jaunty moustache, who smiled at her affectionately.

'Hullo there, young Myra,' he said.

He spoke as if they were old friends, but she had no recollection of ever having seen him before.

'Who are you?' she said. The question seemed abrupt and she wished she had thought of something more polished.

A reproachful look came into his eyes.

'You usedn't to say that when I soaped your back. "Nobody soaps like you, Uncle Fred," you used to say, and you were right. I had the knack.'

The years fell away from Myra, and she was a child in her bath again.

'Well!' she said, squeaking in her emotion.

'I see you remember.'

'Uncle Fred! Fancy meeting you again like this after all these years. Though I suppose I ought to call you Mr Twistleton.'

'You would be making a serious social gaffe, if you did. I've come a long way since we last saw each other. By pluck and industry I've worked my way up the ladder, step by step, to dizzy heights. You may have heard that a Lord Ickenham was expected at the castle today. I am the Lord Ickenham about whom there has been so much talk. And not one of your humble Barons or Viscounts, mind you, but a belted Earl, with papers to prove it.'

'Like Lord Emsworth?'

'Yes, only brighter.'

'I remember now Father saying something about your having become a big wheel.'

'He in no way overstated it. How is he?'

'He's all right.'

'Full of beans?'

'Oh, yes.'

'More than you are, my child. I was watching you sitting there, and you reminded me of Rodin's Penseur. Were you thinking of Bill Bailey?'

Myra started.

'You don't – ?'

'Know Bill Bailey? Certainly I do. He's a friend of my nephew Pongo's and to my mind as fine a curate as ever preached a sermon.'

The animation which had come into the girl's face at this reunion with one of whom she had such pleasant memories died away to be replaced by a cold haughtiness like that of a princess reluctantly compelled to give her attention to the dregs of the underworld.

'You're entitled to your opinion, I suppose,' she said stiffly. 'I think he's a rat.'

It seemed to Lord Ickenham that he could not have heard correctly. Young lovers, he knew, were accustomed to bestow on each other a variety of pet names, but he had never understood 'rat' to be one of them.

'A *rat*?'

'Yes.'

'Why do you call him that?'

'Because of what he did.'

'What was that?'

'Or didn't do, rather.'

'You speak in riddles. Couldn't you make it clearer?'

'I'll make it clearer, all right. He stood me up.'

'I still don't get the gist.'

'Very well, then, if you want the whole story. I phoned him that I was coming to London to marry him, and he didn't show up at the registry office.'

'What!'

'Had cold feet, I suppose. I ought to have guessed from the way he said "Oh, rather", when I asked him if he wasn't pleased. I waited at the place for hours, but he never appeared. And he told me he loved me!'

It was not often that Lord Ickenham was bewildered, but he found himself now unequal to the intellectual pressure of the conversation.

'He never appeared? Are we talking of the same man? The one I mean is an up-and-coming young cleric named Bill Bailey, in whose company I passed fully three-quarters of an hour yesterday at the registry office. I was to have been one of his witnesses, lending a tone to the thing.'

Myra stared.

'Are you crazy?'

'The charge has sometimes been brought against me, but there's nothing in it. Just exuberant. Why do you ask?'

'He can't have been at the registry office. I'd have seen him.'

'He's hard to miss, I agree. Catches the eye, as you might say. But I assure you –'

'At the registry office in Wilton Street?'

'Say that again.'

'Say what again?'

'Wilton Street.'

'Why?'

'I wanted to test a theory that has just occurred to me. I think I have the solution of this mystery that has been perplexing us. Someone, especially if a good deal agitated hearing somebody say "Wilton" over the telephone, could easily mistake it for "Milton". Some trick of the acoustics. It was at the Milton Street registry office that Bill, my nephew Pongo and I kept our vigil. We all missed you.'

The colour drained from Myra Schoonmaker's face. Her eyes, as they stared into Lord Ickenham's, had become almost as prominent as the Duke's.

'You don't mean that?'

'I do, indeed. There were we, waiting at the church –'

'Oh, golly, what an escape I've had!'

Lord Ickenham could not subscribe to this view.

'Now there I disagree with you. My acquaintance with Bill Bailey has been brief, but as I told you, it has left me with a distinctly favourable impression of him. A sterling soul he seemed to me. I feel the spiritual needs of Bottleton East are safe in the hands of a curate like that. Don't tell me you've weakened on him?'

'Of course I've not weakened on him.'

'Then why do you feel that you have had an escape?'

'Because I came back here so mad with him for standing me up, as I thought, that when Archie Gilpin proposed to me I very nearly accepted him.'

Lord Ickenham looked grave. These artists, he was thinking, work fast.

'But you didn't?'

'No.'

'Well, don't. It would spoil Bill's visit. And I want him to enjoy himself at Blandings Castle. But I didn't tell you about that, did I? It must have slipped my mind. I've brought Bill here with me. Incognito, of course. I thought you might like to see him. I always strive, when I can, to spread sweetness and light. There have been several complaints about it.'

CHAPTER FOUR

1

It was the practice of Lord Ickenham, when visiting a country house to look about him, before doing anything else, for a hammock to which he could withdraw after breakfast and lie thinking deep thoughts. Though, like Abou ben Adhem a man who loved his fellow men, he made it an invariable rule to avoid them after the morning meal with an iron firmness, for at that delectable hour he wished to be alone to meditate. Whoever wanted to enjoy the sparkle of his conversation had to wait till lunch, when it would be available to all.

Such a hammock he had found on the lawn of Blandings Castle, and on the morning after his arrival he was reclining in it at peace with all the world. The day was warm and sunny. A breeze blew gently from the west. Birds chirped, bees buzzed, insects droned as they went about the various businesses that engage the attention of insects in the rural districts. In the stable yard, out of view behind a shrubbery, somebody – possibly Voules the chauffeur – was playing the harmonica. And from a window in the house, softened by distance, there sounded faintly the tap-tap-tap of a typewriter, showing that Lavender Briggs, that slave of duty, was at work on some secretarial task and earning the weekly envelope. Soothed and relaxed, Lord Ickenham fell into a reverie.

He had plenty to occupy his mind. As a man who specialized in spreading sweetness and light, he was often confronted with problems difficult of solution, but he had seldom found them so numerous. As he mused on Lady Constance, on Lavender Briggs, on the Duke of Dunstable and on the Church Lads, he could see, as he had told Pongo, that his hands would be full and his ingenuity strained to the uttermost.

He was glad, this being so, that he had not got to worry about Bill Bailey, who had relieved whatever apprehensions he may have had by fitting well into the little Blandings circle. True, Lady Constance had greeted him with a touch of frost in her manner, but that was to be expected. The others, he had been happy to see, had made him welcome, particularly Lord Emsworth, to whom he appeared to have said just the right things about the Empress during yesterday evening's visit to her residence. Lord Emsworth's approval did not, of course, carry much weight at Blandings Castle, but it was something.

It was as he lay meditating on Lord Emsworth that he observed him crossing the lawn and sat up with a start of surprise. What had astonished him was not the other's presence there, for the proprietor of a country house has of course a perfect right to cross lawns on his own premises, but the fact that he was wet. Indeed, the word 'wet' was barely adequate. He was soaked from head to foot and playing like a Versailles fountain.

This puzzled Lord Ickenham. He was aware that his host sometimes took a dip in the lake, but he had not known that he did it immediately after breakfast with all his clothes on, and abandoning his usual policy of allowing nothing to get him out of his hammock till the hour of the midday cocktail, he started in pursuit.

Lord Emsworth was cutting out a good pace, so good that he remained out of earshot, and he had disappeared into the house before Lord Ickenham reached it. The latter, shrewdly reasoning that a wet man would make for his bedroom, followed him there. He found him in the nude, drying himself with a bath towel, and immediately put the question which would have occurred to anyone in his place.

'My dear fellow, what happened? Did you fall into the lake?'

Lord Emsworth lowered the towel and reached for a patched shirt.

'Eh? Oh, hullo, Ickenham. Did you say you had fallen into the lake?'

'I asked if you had.'

'I? Oh, no.'

'Don't tell me that was merely perspiration you were bathed in when I saw you on the lawn?'

'Eh? No, I perspire very little. But I did not fall into the lake. I dived in.'

'With your clothes on?'

'Yes, I had my clothes on.'

'Any particular reason for diving? Or did it just seem a good idea at the time?'

'I had lost my glasses.'

'And you thought they might be in the lake?'

Lord Emsworth appeared to realize that he had not made himself altogether clear. For some moments he busied himself with a pair of trousers. Having succeeded in draping his long legs in these, he explained.

'No, it was not that. But when I am without my glasses, I find a difficulty in seeing properly. And I had no reason to suppose that the boy was not accurate in his statement.'

'What boy was that?'

'One of the Church Lads. I spoke to you about them, if you remember.'

'I remember.'

'I wish somebody would mend my socks,' said Lord Emsworth, deviating for a moment from the main theme. 'Look at those holes. What were we talking about?'

'This statement-making Church Lad.'

'Oh yes. Yes, quite. Well, the whole thing was very peculiar. I had gone down to the lake with the idea of asking the boys if they could possibly make a little less noise, and suddenly one of them came running up to me with the most extraordinary remark. He said, "Oh, sir, please save Willie!"'

'Odd way of starting a conversation, certainly.'

'He was pointing at an object in the water, and putting two and two together I came to the conclusion that one of his comrades must have fallen into the lake and was drowning. So I dived in.'

Lord Ickenham was impressed.

'Very decent of you. Many men who had suffered so much at the hands of the little blisters would just have stood on the bank and sneered. Was the boy grateful?'

'I can't find my shoes. Oh yes, here they are. What did you say?'

'Did the boy thank you brokenly?'

'What boy?'

'The one whose life you saved.'

'Oh, I was going to explain that. It wasn't a boy. It turned out to be a floating log. I swam to it, shouting to it to keep cool, and was very much annoyed to find that my efforts had been for nothing. And do you know what I think, Ickenham? I strongly suspect that it was not a genuine mistake on the boy's part. I am convinced that he was perfectly well aware that the object in the water was not one of his playmates and that he had deliberately deceived me. Oh yes, I feel sure of it, and I'll tell you why. When I came out, he had been joined by several other boys, and they were laughing.'

Lord Ickenham could readily imagine it. They would, he supposed, be laughing when they told the story to their grandchildren.

'I asked them what they were laughing at, and they said it was at something funny which had happened on the previous afternoon. I found it hard to credit their story.'

'I don't wonder.'

'I feel very indignant about the whole affair.'

'I'm not surprised.'

'Should I complain to Constance?'

'I think I would do something more spirited than that.'

'But what?'

'Ah, that wants thinking over, doesn't it? I'll devote earnest thought to the matter, and if anything occurs to me, I'll let you know. You wouldn't consider mowing them down with a shotgun?'

'Eh? No, I doubt if that would be advisable.'

'Might cause remark, you feel?' said Lord Ickenham. 'Perhaps you're right. Never mind. I'll think of something else.'

When a visitor to a country house learns that his host, as to the stability of whose mental balance he has long entertained the gravest doubts, has suddenly jumped into a lake with all his clothes on, he cannot but feel concern. He shakes his head. He purses his lips and raises his eyebrows. Something has given, he says to himself, and strains have been cracked under. It was thus that the Duke of Dunstable reacted to the news of Lord Emsworth's exploit.

It was from the latter's grandson George that he got the story. George was a small boy with ginger hair and freckles, and between him and the Duke there had sprung up one of those odd friendships which do sometimes spring up between the most unlikely persons. George was probably the only individual in three counties who actually enjoyed conversing with the Duke of Dunstable. If he had been asked wherein lay the other's fascination, he would have replied that he liked watching the way he blew his moustache about when he talked. It was a spectacle that never wearied him.

'I say,' he said, coming on to the terrace where the Duke was sitting, 'have you heard the latest?'

The Duke, who had been brooding on the seeming impossibility of getting an egg boiled the way he liked it in this blasted house, came out of his thoughts. He spoke irritably. Owing to his tender years George had rather a high voice, and the sudden sound of it had made him bite his tongue.

'Don't come squeaking in my ear like that, boy. Blow your horn or something. What did you say?'

'I asked if you'd heard the latest?'

'Latest what?'

'Front page news. Big scoop. Grandpapa jumped into the lake.'

'What are you talking about?'

'It's true. The country's ringing with it. I had it from one of the gardeners who saw him. Grandpapa was walking along by the lake, and suddenly he stopped and paused for a moment in thought. Then he did a swan dive,' said George, and eyed the moustache expectantly.

He was not disappointed. It danced like an autumn leaf before a gale.

'He jumped into the lake?'

'That's what he did, big boy.'

'Don't call me big boy.'

'Okay, chief.'

The Duke puffed awhile.

'You say this gardener saw him jump into the water?'

'Yes, *sir*.'

'With his clothes on?'

'That's right. Accoutred as he was, he plunged in,' said George, who in the preceding term at his school had had to write out a familiar passage from Shakespeare's *Julius Caesar* fifty times for bringing a white mouse into the classroom. 'Pretty sporting, don't you think, an old egg like Grandpapa?'

'What do you mean – old egg?'

'Well, he must be getting on for a hundred.'

'He is the same age as myself.'

'Oh?' said George, who supposed the Duke had long since passed the hundred mark.

'But what the deuce made him do a thing like that?'

'Oh, just thought he would, I suppose. Coo – I wish I'd been there with my camera,' said George, and went on his way.

And a few moments later, having pondered deeply on this sensational development, the Duke rose and stumped off in search of Lady Constance. What he had heard convinced him of the need for a summit meeting.

He found her in her sitting-room. Lavender Briggs was with her, all spectacles and notebook. It was part of her secretarial duties to look in at this hour for general instructions.

'Hoy!' he boomed like something breaking the sound barrier.

'Oh, Alaric!' said Lady Constance, startled and annoyed. 'I do wish you would knock.'

'Less of the "Oh, Alaric!"' said the Duke, who was always firm with this sort of thing, 'and where's the sense in knocking? I want to talk to you on a matter of the utmost importance, and it's private. Pop off, you,' he said to Lavender Briggs. He was a man who had a short way with underlings. 'It's about Emsworth.'

'What about him?'

'I'll tell you what about him, just as soon as this pie-faced female has removed herself. Don't want her muscling in with her ears sticking up, hearing every word I say.'

'You had better leave us, Miss Briggs.'

'Quate,' said Lavender Briggs, withdrawing haughtily.

'Really, Alaric,' said Lady Constance as the door closed, speaking with the frankness of one who had known him for a lifetime, 'you have the manners of a pig.'

The Duke reacted powerfully to the criticism. He banged the desk with a hamlike hand, upsetting, in the order named, an inkpot, two framed photographs and a vase of roses.

'Pig! That's the operative word. It's the pig I came to talk about.'

Lady Constance would have preferred to talk about the inkpot, the two photographs and the vase of roses, but he gave her no opportunity. He had always been a difficult man to stop.

'It's at the bottom of the whole thing. It's a thoroughly bad influence on him. Stop messing about with that ink and listen to me. I say it's the pig that has made him what he is today.'

'Oh, dear! Made whom what he is today?'

'Emsworth, of course, ass. Who do you think I meant? Constance,' said the Duke in that loud, carrying voice of his, 'I've told you this before, and I tell it to you again. If Emsworth is to be saved from the loony bin, that pig must be removed from his life.'

'Don't shout so, Alaric.'

'I will shout. I feel very strongly on the matter. The pig is affecting his brain, not that he ever had much. Remember the time when he told me he wanted to enter it for the Derby?'

'I spoke to him about that. He said he didn't.'

'Well, I say he did! Heard him distinctly. Anyway, be that as it may, you can't deny that he's half way round the bend, and I maintain that the pig is responsible. It's at the root of his mental unbalance.'

'Clarence is not mentally unbalanced!'

'He isn't, isn't he? That's what you think. How about what happened this morning? You know the lake?'

'Of course I know the lake.'

'He was walking beside it.'

'Why shouldn't he walk beside the lake?'

'I'm not saying he shouldn't walk beside the lake. He can walk beside the lake till his eyes bubble, as far as I'm concerned. But when it comes to jumping in with all his clothes on, it makes one think a bit.'

'What!'

'That's what he did, so young George informs me.'

'With his *clothes* on?'

'Accoutred as he was.'

'Well, really!'

'Don't know why you seem surprised. It didn't surprise me. I was saddened, yes, but not surprised. Been expecting something like this for a long time. It's just the sort of thing a man would do whose intellect had been sapped by constant association with a pig. And that's why I tell you that the pig must go. Eliminate it, and all may still be well. I'm not saying that anything could make Emsworth actually sane, one mustn't expect miracles, but I'm convinced that if he hadn't this pig to unsettle him all the time, you would see a marked improvement. He'd be an altogether brighter, less potty man. Well, say something, woman. Don't just sit there. Take steps, take steps.'

'What steps?'

'Slip somebody a couple of quid to smuggle the ghastly animal away somewhere, thus removing Emsworth from its sphere of influence.'

'My dear Alaric!'

'It's the only course to pursue. He won't sell the creature, though if I've asked him once, I've asked him a dozen times. "I'll give you five hundred pounds cash down for that bulbous mass of lard and snuffle," I said to him. "Say the word," I said, "and I'll have the revolting object shipped off right away to my place in Wiltshire, paying all the expenses of removal." He refused, and was offensive about it, too. The man's besotted.'

'But you don't keep pigs.'

'I know I don't, not such a silly ass, but I'm prepared to pay five hundred pounds for this one.'

Lady Constance's eyes widened.

'Just to do Clarence good?' she said, amazed. She had not credited her guest with this altruism.

'Certainly not,' said the Duke, offended that he should be supposed capable of any such motive. 'I can make a bit of money out of it. I know someone who'll give me two thousand for the animal.'

'Good gracious! Who . . . Oh, Clarence!'

Lord Emsworth had burst into the room, plainly in the grip of some strong emotion. His mild eyes were gleaming through their pince-nez, and he quivered like a tuning-fork.

'Connie,' he cried, and you could see that he had been pushed just so far. 'You've got to do something about these infernal boys!'

Lady Constance sighed wearily. This was one of those trying mornings.

'What boys? Do you mean the Church Lads?'

'Eh? Yes, precisely. They should never have been let into the place. What do you think I just found one of them doing? He was leaning over the rail of Empress's sty, where he had no business to be, and he was dangling a potato on a string in front of her nose and jerking it away when she snapped at it. Might have ruined her digestion for days. You've got to do something about it, Constance. The boy must be apprehended and severely punished.'

'Oh, Clarence!'

'I insist. He must be given a sharp lesson.'

'Changing the subject,' said the Duke, 'will you sell me that foul pig of yours? I'll give you six hundred pounds.'

Lord Emsworth stared at him, revolted. His eyes glowed hotly behind their pince-nez. Not even George Cyril Wellbeloved could have disliked dukes more.

'Of course I won't. I've told you a dozen times. Nothing would induce me to sell the Empress.'

'Six hundred pounds. That's a firm offer!'

'I don't want six hundred pounds. I've got plenty of money, plenty.'

'Clarence,' said Lady Constance, also changing the subject, 'is it true that you jumped into the lake this morning with all your clothes on?'

'Eh? What? Yes, certainly. I couldn't wait to take them off. Only it was a log.'

'What was a log?'

'The boy.'

'What boy?'

'The log. But I can't stand here talking,' said Lord Emsworth impatiently, and hurried out, turning at the door to repeat to Lady Constance that she must do something about it.

The Duke blew his moustache up a few inches.

'You see? What did I tell you? Definitely barmy. Reached the gibbering stage, and may get dangerous at any moment. But I was speaking about this fellow who'll give two thousand for the porker. I used to know him years ago when I was a young man in London. Pyke was his name then. Stinker Pyke we used to call him. Then he made a packet by running all those papers and magazines and things and got a peerage. Calls himself Lord Tilbury now. You've met him. He says he's stayed here.'

'Yes, he was here for a short time. My brother Galahad used

to know him. Miss Briggs was his secretary before she came to us.'

'I'm not interested in Miss Briggs, blast her spectacles.'

'I merely mentioned it.'

'Well, don't mention it again. Now you've made me forget what I was going to tell you. Oh, yes. I ran into Stinker at the club the other day, and we got talking and I said I was coming to Blandings, and the subject of the pig came up. It appears that he keeps pigs at his place in Buckinghamshire, just the sort of potty thing he would do, and he has coveted this ghastly animal of Emsworth's ever since he saw it. He specifically told me that he would give me two thousand pounds to add it to his piggery.'

'How extraordinary!'

'Opportunity of a lifetime.'

'Clarence must be made to see reason.'

'Who's going to make him? I can't. You heard him just now. And you won't pinch the creature. The thing's an impasse. No co-operation, that's what's wrong with this damned place. Very doubtful if I'll ever come here again. You'll miss me, but that can't be helped. Only yourself to blame. I'm going for a walk,' said the Duke, and proceeded to do so.

3

Lord Emsworth was a man with little of the aggressor in his spiritual make-up. He believed in living and letting live. Except for his sister Constance, his secretary Lavender Briggs, the Duke of Dunstable and his younger son Frederick, now fortunately residing in America, few things were able to ruffle him. Placid is the word that springs to the lips.

But the Church Lads had pierced his armour, and he found resentment growing within him like some shrub that has been treated with a patent fertilizer. He brooded bleakly on the injuries he had suffered at the hands of these juvenile delinquents.

The top-hat incident he could have overlooked, for he knew that when small boys are confronted with a man wearing that type of headgear and there is a crusty roll within reach, they are almost bound to lose their calm judgment. The happy laughter which had greeted him as he emerged from the lake had gashed him like a knife, but with a powerful effort he might have excused it. But in upsetting Empress of Blandings' delicately attuned digestive system by dangling potatoes before her eyes and jerking them away as she snapped at them they had gone too far. As Hamlet would have put it, their offence was rank and smelled to heaven. And if heaven would not mete out retribution to them – and there was not a sign so far of any activity in the front office – somebody else would have to attend to it. And that somebody, he was convinced, was Ickenham. He had left Ickenham pondering on the situation, and who knew that by this time his fertile mind might not have hit on a suitable method of vengeance.

On leaving Lady Constance's boudoir, accordingly, he made his way to the hammock and bleated his story into the other's ear. Nor was he disappointed in its reception. Where a man of coarser fibre might have laughed, Lord Ickenham was gravity itself. By not so much as a twitch of the lip did he suggest that he found anything amusing in his host's narrative.

'A potato?' he said, knitting his brow.

'A large potato.'

'On a string?'

'Yes, on a string.'

'And the boy jerked it away?'

'Repeatedly. It must have distressed the Empress greatly. She is passionately fond of potatoes.'

'And you wish to retaliate? You think that something in the nature of a counter move is required?'

'Eh? Yes, certainly.'

'Then how very fortunate,' said Lord Ickenham heartily, 'that I can put you in the way of making it. I throw it out merely as a suggestion, you understand, but I know what I would do in your place.'

'What is that?'

'I'd bide my time and sneak down to the lake in the small hours of the morning and cut the ropes of their tent, as one used to do at the Public Schools Camp at Aldershot in the brave days when I was somewhat younger. That, to my mind, would be the retort courteous.'

'God bless my soul!' said Lord Emsworth.

He spoke with sudden animation. Forty-six years had rolled away from him, the forty-six years which had passed since, a junior member of the Eton contingent at the Aldershot camp, he had been mixed up in that sort of thing. Then he had been on the receiving, not the giving, end. Some young desperadoes from a school allergic to Eton had cut the ropes of the guard tent in which he was reposing, and he could recall vividly his emotions on suddenly finding himself entangled in a cocoon of canvas. His whole life – some fifteen years at that time – had passed before him, and in suggesting a similar experience for these Church Lads Ickenham, he realized, had shown his usual practical good sense.

For a moment his mild face glowed. Then the light died out

of it. Would it, he was asking himself, be altogether prudent to embark on an enterprise of which Connie must inevitably disapprove? Connie had an uncanny knack of finding out things, and if she were to trace this righteous act of vengeance to him . . .

'I'll turn it over in my mind,' he said. 'Thank you very much for the suggestion.'

'Not at all,' said Lord Ickenham. 'Ponder on it at your leisure.'

CHAPTER FIVE

The Duke's walk took him to the Empress's sty, and he lit a cigar and stood leaning on the rail, gazing at her as she made a late breakfast.

Except for a certain fullness of figure, the Duke of Dunstable and Empress of Blandings had little in common. There was no fusion between their souls. The next ten minutes accordingly saw nothing in the nature of an exchange of ideas. The Duke smoked his cigar in silence, the Empress in her single-minded way devoted herself to the consumption of her daily nourishment amounting to fifty-seven thousand five hundred calories.

Lord Emsworth would not have believed such a thing possible, but the spectacle of this supreme pig was plunging the Duke in gloom. It was not with admiration that he gazed upon her, but with a growing fury. There, he was saying to himself, golloped a Berkshire sow which, if conveyed to his Wiltshire home, would mean a cool two thousand pounds added to his bank balance, and no hope of conveying her. The thought was like a dagger in his heart.

His cigar having reached the point where, if persevered

with, it would burn his moustache, he threw it away, straightened himself with a peevish grunt and was about to leave the noble animal to her proteids and carbohydrates, when a voice said 'Pahdon me', and turning he perceived the pie-faced female whom he had so recently put in her place.

'Get out of here!' he said in his polished way, 'I'm busy.'

Where a lesser woman would have quailed and beaten an apologetic retreat, Lavender Briggs stood firm, her dignified calm unruffled. No man, however bald his head or white his moustache, could intimidate a girl who had served under the banner of Lord Tilbury of the Mammoth Publishing Company.

'I would like a word with Your Grace,' she said in the quiet, level voice which only an upbringing in Kensington followed by years of secretarial college can produce. 'It is with refahrence,' she went on, ignoring the purple flush which had crept over her companion's face, 'to this pig of Lord Emsworth's. I chanced to overhear what you were saying to Lady Constance just now.'

A cascade of hair dashed itself against the Duke's Wellingtonian nose.

'Eavesdropping, eh? Listening at keyholes, what?'

'Quate,' said Lavender Briggs, unmoved by the acidity of his tone. In her time she had been spoken acidly to by experts. 'You were urging Lady Constance to pay somebody to purloin the animal. To which her reply' – she consulted a shorthand note in her notebook – 'was "My dear Alaric!", indicating that she was not prepare-ahed to consid-ah the idea-h. Had you made the suggestion to me, you would not have received such a dusty answer.'

'Such a what?'

A contemptuous light flickered for an instant behind the harlequin glasses. Lavender Briggs moved in circles where literary allusions were grabbed off the bat, and the other's failure to get his hands to this one aroused her scorn. She did not actually call the Duke an ill-read old bohunkus, but this criticism was implicit in the way she looked at him.

'A quotation. "Ah, what a dusty answer gets the soul when hot for certainties in this our life." George Meredith, "Modern Love," stanza forty-eight.'

The Duke's head had begun to swim a little, but with the sensation of slight giddiness had come an unwilling respect for this goggled girl. Superficially all that stanza forty-eight stuff might seem merely another indication of the pottiness which was so marked a feature of the other sex, but there was something in her manner that suggested that she had more to say and that eventually something would emerge that made sense. This feeling solidified as she proceeded.

'If we can came to some satisfactory business arrangement, I will abstract the pig and see that it is delivered at your address.'

The Duke blinked. Whatever he had been expecting, it was not this. He looked at the Empress, estimating her tonnage, then at Lavender Briggs, in comparison so fragile.

'You? Don't be an ass. You couldn't steal a pig.'

'I should, of course, engage the service of an assistant to do the rough work.'

'Who? Not me.'

'I was not thinking of Your Grace.'

'Then who?'

'I would prefer not to specify with any greatah exactitude.'

'See what you mean. No names, no pack-drill?'

'Quate.'

A thoughtful silence fell. Lavender Briggs stood looking like a spectacled statue, while the Duke, who had lighted another cigar, puffed at it. And at this moment Lord Emsworth appeared, walking across the meadow in that jerky way of his which always reminded his friends and admirers of a mechanical toy which had been insufficiently wound up.

'Hell!' said the Duke. 'Here comes Emsworth.'

'Quate,' said Lavender Briggs. It was obvious to her that the conference must be postponed to some more suitable time and place. Above all else, plotters require privacy. 'I suggest that Your Grace meet me later in my office.'

'Where's that?'

'Beach will direct you.'

The secretary's office, to which the butler some quarter of an hour later escorted the Duke, was at the far end of a corridor, a small room looking out on the Dutch garden. Like herself, it was tidy and austere, with no fripperies. There was a desk with a typewriter on it, a table with a tape-recording machine on it, filing cabinets against the walls, a chair behind the desk, another chair in front of it, both hard and business-like, and – the sole concession to the beautiful – a bowl of flowers by the window. As the Duke entered, she was sitting in the chair behind the desk, and he, after eyeing it suspiciously as if doubtful of its ability to support the largest trouser-seat in the peerage, took the other chair.

'Been thinking over what you were saying just now,' he said. 'About stealing that pig for me. This assistant you were speaking of. Sure you can get him?'

'I am. Actually, I shall requiah two assistants.'

'Eh?'

'One to push and one to pull. It is a very large pig.'

'Oh, yes, see what you mean. Yes, undoubtedly. As you say, very large pig. And you can get this second chap?'

'I can.'

'Good. Then that seems to be about it, what? Everything settled, I mean to say.'

'Except terms.'

'Eh?'

'If you will recall, I spoke of a satisfactory business arrangement? I naturally expect to be compensated for my services. I am anxious to obtain capital with which to start a typewriting bureau.'

The Duke, a prudent man who believed in watching the pennies, said, 'A typewriting bureau, eh? I know the sort of thing you mean. One of those places full of machines and girls hammering away at them like a lot of dashed riveters. Well, you don't want much money for that,' he said, and Lavender Briggs, correcting this view, said she wanted as much as she could get.

'I would suggest five hundred pounds.'

The Duke's moustache leaped into life. His eyes bulged. He had the air of one who is running the gamut of the emotions.

'Five . . . *what?*'

'You were thinking of some lesser fig-ah?'

'I was thinking of a tenner.'

'Ten pounds?' Lavender Briggs smiled pityingly, as if some acquaintance of hers, quoting Horace, had made a false quantity. 'That would leave you with a nice profit, would it not?'

'Eh?'

'You told Lady Constance that you had a friend who was prepared to pay you two thousand pounds for the animal.'

The Duke chewed his moustache in silence for a moment, regretting that he had been so explicit.

'I was pulling her leg,' he said, doing his best.

'Oh?'

'Harmless little joke.'

'Indeed? I took it au pied de la lettre.'

'Au what de what?' said the Duke, who was as shaky on French as he was on English literature.

'I accepted the statement at its face value.'

'Silly of you. Thought you would have seen that I was just kidding her along and making a good story out of it.'

'That was not the impression your words made on me. When' – she consulted her notebook – 'when I heard you say "I know someone who'll give me two thousand for the animal", I was quate convinced that you meant precisely what you said. Unfortunately at that moment Lord Emsworth appeared and I was obliged to move from the door, so did not ascertain the name of the friend to whom you referred. Otherwise, I would be dealing with him directly and you would not appear in the transaction at all. As matters stand, you will be receiving fifteen hundred pounds for doing nothing – from your point of view, I should have supposed, a very satisfactory state of aff-ay-ars.'

She became silent. She was thinking hard thoughts of Lord Emsworth and feeling how like him it was to have intruded at such a vital moment. Had he postponed his arrival for as little as half a minute, she would have learned the identity of this lavish pig-lover and would have been able to dispense with the middle man. A momentary picture rose before her eyes of herself, armed with a stout umbrella, taking a full back swing and breaking it over her employer's head. Even though she recognized this as but an idle dream, it comforted her a little.

The Duke sat chewing his cigar. There was, he had to admit, much in what she said. The thought of parting with five hundred pounds chilled him to his parsimonious marrow, but after all, as she had indicated, the remaining fifteen hundred was nice money and would come under the general heading of velvet.

'All right,' he said, though it hurt him to utter the words, and Lavender Briggs' mouth twitched slightly on the left side, which was her way of smiling.

'I was sure you would be reasonable. Shall we have a written agreement?'

'No,' said the Duke, remembering that one of the few sensible remarks his late father had ever made was 'Alaric, my boy, never put anything in writing'. 'No, certainly not. Written agreement, indeed! Never heard a pottier suggestion in my life.'

'Then I must ask you for a cheque.'

As far as it is possible for a seated man to do so, the Duke reeled.

'What, in advance?'

'Quate. Have you your cheque-book with you?'

'No,' said the Duke, brightening momentarily. For an instant it seemed to him that this solved everything.

'Then you can give it me tonight,' said Lavender Briggs. 'And meanwhile repeat this after me. I, Alaric, Duke of Dunstable, hereby make a solemn promise to you, Lavender Briggs, that if you steal Lord Emsworth's pig, Empress of

Blandings, and deliver it to my home in Wiltshire, I will pay you the sum of five hundred pounds.'

'Sounds silly.'

'Nevertheless, I must insist on a formal agreement, even if only a verbal one.'

'Oh, all right.'

The Duke repeated the words, though still considering them silly. The woman had to be humoured.

'Thank you,' said Lavender Briggs, and went off to scour the countryside for George Cyril Wellbeloved.

2

George Cyril was having his elevenses in the tool-shed by the kitchen garden when the rich smell of pig which he always diffused enabled her eventually to locate him. As she entered, closing the door behind her, he lowered the beer bottle from his lips in some surprise. He had seen her around from time to time and knew who she was, but he had not the pleasure of her acquaintance, and he was wondering to what he owed the honour of this visit.

She informed him, but not immediately, for there was what are called pourparlers to be gone through first.

'Wellbeloved,' she said, starting to attend to these, 'I have been making inquiries about you in Market Blandings, and everyone to whom I have mentioned your name tells me that you are thoroughly untrustworthy, a man without scruples of any sort, who sticks at nothing and will do anything for money.'

'Who – me?' said George Cyril, blinking. He had frequently had much the same sort of thing said to him before, for he moved in outspoken circles, but somehow it seemed worse and more wounding coming from those Kensingtonian lips. For a moment he debated within himself the advisability of dotting the speaker one on the boko, but decided against this. You never know what influential friends these women had. He contented himself with waving his arms in a passionate gesture which caused the aroma of pig to spread itself even more thickly about the interior of the shed. 'Who – me?' he said again.

Lavender Briggs had produced a scented handkerchief and was pressing it to her face.

'Toothache?' asked George Cyril, interested.

'It is a little close in here,' said Lavender Briggs primly, and returned to the pourparlers. 'At the Emsworth Arms, for instance, I was informed that you would sell your grandmother for twopence.'

George Cyril said he did not have a grandmother, and seemed a good deal outraged by the suggestion that, if that relative had not long since gone to reside with the morning stars, he would have parted with her at such bargain-basement rates. A good grandmother should fetch at least a couple of bob.

'At the Cow and Grasshopper they told me you were a – petty thief of the lowest description.'

'Who – me?' said George Cyril uneasily. That, he told himself, must be those cigars. He had not supposed that suspicion had fallen on himself regarding their disappearance. Evidently the hand had not moved sufficiently quickly to deceive the eye.

'And the butler at Sir Gregory Parsloe's, where I understand you were employed before you returned to Lord Emsworth, said you were always pilfering his cigarettes and whisky.'

'Who – me?' said George Cyril for the fourth time, speaking now with an outraged note in his voice. He had always thought of Binstead, Sir Gregory's butler, as a pal and, what is more, a staunch pal. And now this. Like the prophet Zachariah, he was saying to himself, 'I have been wounded in the house of my friends.'

'Your moral standards have thus been established as negligible. So I want you,' said Lavender Briggs, 'to steal Lord Emsworth's pig.'

Another man, hearing these words, might have been stunned, and certainly a fifth 'Who – me?' could have been expected, but in making this request of George Cyril Wellbeloved the secretary was addressing one who in the not distant past actually had stolen Lord Emsworth's pig. It was a long and intricate story, reflecting great discredit on all concerned, and there is no need to go into it now. One mentions it merely to explain why George Cyril Wellbeloved did not draw himself to his full height and thunder that nothing could make him betray his position of trust, but merely scratched his chin with the beer bottle and looked interested.

'Pinch the pig?'

'Precisely.'

'Why?'

'Never mind why?'

George Cyril did mind why.

'Now use your intelligence, miss,' he pleaded. 'You can't come telling a man to go pinching pigs without giving him the griff about why he's doing it and who for and what not. Who's after that pig this time?'

Lavender Briggs decided to be frank. She was a fair-minded

girl and saw that he had reason on his side. Even the humblest hired assassin in the Middle Ages probably wanted to know, before setting out to stick a poignard into someone, whom he was acting for.

'The Duke of Dunstable,' she said. 'You would be requiahed to take the animal to his house in Wiltshire.'

'Wiltshire?' George Cyril seemed incredulous. 'Did you say Wiltshire?'

'That is where the Duke lives.'

'And how do we get to Wiltshire, me and the pig? Walk?'

Lavender Briggs clicked her tongue impatiently.

'I assume that you have some disreputable friend who has a motor vehicle of some kind and is as free from scruples as yourself. And if you are thinking that you may be suspected, you need have no uneasiness. The operation will be carried through early in the morning and nobody will suppose that you were not asleep in bed at the time.'

George Cyril nodded. This was talking sense.

'Yes, so far so good. But aren't you overlooking what I might call a technical point? I can't pinch a pig that size all by myself.'

'You will have a colleague, working with you.'

'I will?'

'Quate.'

'Who pays him?'

'He will not requiah payment.'

'Must be barmy. All right, then, we've got that straight. We now come to the financial aspect of the thing. To speak expleasantly, what is there in it for me?'

'Five pounds.'

'*Five?*'

'Let us say ten.'

'Let us ruddy well say fifty.'

'That is a lot of money.'

'I like a lot of money.'

It was a moment for swift decisions. Lavender Briggs shared the Duke's views on watching the pennies, but she was a realist and knew that if you do not speculate, you cannot accumulate.

'Very well. No doubt I can persuade the Duke to meet you on the point. He is a rich man.'

'R!' said George Cyril Wellbeloved, so far forgetting himself as to spit out of the side of his mouth. 'And how did he get his riches? By grinding the face of the poor and taking the bread out of the mouths of the widow and the orphan. But the red dawn will come,' he said, warming up to his subject. 'One of these days you'll see blood flowing in streams down Park Lane and the corpses of the oppressors hanging from lamp-posts. And His Nibs of Dunstable'll be one of them. And who'll be there, pulling on the rope? Me, and happy to do it.'

Lavender Briggs made no comment on this. She was not interested in her companion's plans for the future, though in principle she approved of suspending Dukes from lamp-posts. All she was thinking at the moment was that she had concluded a most satisfactory business deal, and like a good business girl she was feeling quietly elated. She stood to make four hundred and fifty pounds instead of five hundred, but then she had always foreseen that there would be overheads.

The conference having been concluded and terms arranged, George Cyril Wellbeloved felt justified in raising the beer bottle to his lips, and the spectacle reminded her that there was something else that must be added.

'There is just one thing,' she said. 'No more fuddling yourself with alcoholic liquor. This is a very delicate operation which you will be undertaking, and we cannot risk failure. I want you bright and alert. So no more drinking.'

'Except beer, of course.'

'No beer.'

If George Cyril had not been sitting on an upturned wheelbarrow, he would have reeled.

'No beer?'

'No beer.'

'When you say no beer, do you mean no *beer*?'

'Quate. I shall be keeping an eye on you, and I have my way of finding out things. If I discover that you have been drinking, you will lose your fifty pounds. Do I make myself clear?'

'Quate,' said George Cyril Wellbeloved gloomily.

'Then that is understood,' said Lavender Briggs. 'Keep it well in mind.'

She left the shed, glad to escape from its somewhat cloying atmosphere, and started to return to the house. She was anxious now to have a word with Lord Ickenham's friend Cuthbert Meriwether.

3

Lying in his hammock, a soothing cigarette between his lips and his mind busy with great thoughts, Lord Ickenham became aware of emotional breathing in his rear and realized with annoyance that his privacy had been invaded. Then the breather came within the orbit of his vision and he saw that it was not, as for an instant he had feared, the Duke of

Dunstable, but only his young friend, Myra Schoonmaker. He had no objection to suspending his thinking in order to converse with Myra.

It seemed to him, as he rose courteously, that the child was steamed up about something. Her eyes were wild, and there was in her manner a suggestion of the hart panting for cooling streams when heated in the chase. And her first words told him that his diagnosis had been correct.

'Oh, Uncle Fred! The most awful thing has happened!'

He patted her shoulder soothingly. Those who brought their troubles to him always caught him at his best. Such was his magic that there had been times – though not on the occasion of their visit to the dog races – when he had even been able to still the fluttering nervous system of his nephew Pongo.

'Take a hammock, my dear, and tell me all about it,' he said. 'You mustn't let yourself get so agitated. I have no doubt that when we go into it we shall find that whatever is disturbing you is simply the ordinary sort of thing you have to expect when you come to Blandings Castle. As you have probably discovered for yourself by now, Blandings Castle is no place for weaklings. What's on your mind?'

'It's Bill.'

'What has Bill been doing?'

'It's not what he's been doing, poor lamb, it's what's being done to him. You know that secretary woman?'

'Lavender Briggs? We're quite buddies. Emsworth doesn't like her, but for me she has a rather gruesome charm. She reminds me of the dancing mistress at my first kindergarten, on whom I had a crush in my formative years. Though when I say crush, it wasn't love exactly, more a sort of awed respect. I feel the same about Lavender Briggs. I had a long chat with her the other day. She was telling me she wanted to start a typewriting bureau, but hadn't enough capital. Why she should have confided in me, I don't know. I suppose I have one of those rare sympathetic natures you hear about. A cynic would probably say that she was leading up to trying to make a touch, but I don't think so. I think it was simply . . . Swedish exercises?' he asked, breaking off, for his companion had flung her arms out in a passionate gesture.

'Don't *talk* so much, Uncle Fred!'

Lord Ickenham felt the justice of the rebuke. He apologized.

'I'm sorry. A bad habit of mine, which I will endeavour to correct. What were you going to say about La Briggs?'

'She's a loathsome blackmailer!'

'She's *what*? You astound me. Who – or, rather, whom – is she blackmailing?'

'Bill, the poor angel. She's told him he's got to steal Lord Emsworth's pig.'

It took a great deal to make Lord Ickenham start. These words, however, did so. The rule by which he lived his life was that the prudent man, especially when at Blandings Castle, should be ready at all times for anything, but he had certainly not been prepared for this. His was a small moustache, not bushy and billowy like the Duke's, and it did not leap as the Duke's would have done, but it quivered perceptibly. He stared at his young friend as at a young friend who has had a couple.

'What on earth do you mean?'

'I'm telling you. She says Bill has got to steal Lord Emsworth's pig. I don't know who's behind her, but somebody wants it and she's working for him, and she's drafted my poor darling Bill as her assistant.'

Lord Ickenham whistled softly. Never a dull moment at Blandings castle, he was thinking. At first incredulous, he now saw how plausible the girl's story was. People who employ people to steal pigs know that the labourer is worthy of his hire, and the principal in this venture, whoever he was, would undoubtedly reward Lavender Briggs with a purse of gold, thus enabling her to start her typewriting bureau. All that was plain enough, and one could understand the Briggs enthusiasm for the project, but there remained the perplexing problem of why she had selected the Rev Cuthbert Bailey as her collaborator. Why, dash it, thought Lord Ickenham, they hardly knew one another.

'But why Bill?'

'You mean Why *Bill*?'

'Exactly. Why is he the people's choice?'

'Because she's got the goods on him. Shall I tell you the whole thing?'

'It would be a great help.'

Prefacing her remarks with the statement that if girls like Lavender Briggs were skinned alive and dipped in boiling oil, this would be a better and sweeter world, Myra embarked on her narrative.

'Bill was out taking a stroll just now, and she came along. He said, "Oh, hello. Nice morning."'

'And she said "Quate"?'

'No, she said, "I should like a word with you, Mr Bailey."'

'Mr *Bailey*? She knew who he was?'

'She's known from the moment he got here. Apparently when she lived in London, she used to mess about in Bottleton

East, doing good works among the poor and all that, so of course she saw him there and recognized him when he showed up at the castle. Bill's is the sort of face one remembers.'

Lord Ickenham agreed that it did indeed stamp itself on the mental retina. He was looking grave. Expecting at the outset to be called on to deal with some trifling girlish malaise, probably imaginary, he saw that here was a major crisis. If defied, he realized, Lavender Briggs would at once take Lady Constance into her confidence, with the worst results. Hell has no fury like a woman scorned, and very few like a woman who finds that she has been tricked into entertaining at her home a curate at the thought of whom she has been shuddering for weeks. Unquestionably Lady Constance would take umbrage. There would be pique on her part, and even dudgeon, and Bill's visit to Blandings Castle would be abruptly curtailed. In a matter of minutes the unfortunate young pastor of souls would be slung out of this Paradise on his ear like Lucifer, son of the morning.

'And then?'

'She said he had got to steal the pig.'

'And what did he say?'

'He told her to go to hell.'

'Strange advice from a curate.'

'I'm just giving you the rough idea.'

'Quate.'

'Actually, he said Lord Emsworth was his host and had been very kind to him, and he was very fond of him and he'd be darned if he'd bring his grey hairs in sorrow to the grave by pinching his pig, and apart from that what would his bishop have to say, if the matter was drawn to his attention?'

Lord Ickenham nodded.

'One sees what he meant. Curates must watch their step. One false move, like being caught stealing pigs, and bang goes any chance they may have had of rising to become Princes of the Church. And she −?'

'Told him to think it over, the −'

Lord Ickenham raised a hand.

'I know the word that is trembling on your lips, child, but don't utter it. Let us keep the conversation at as high a level as possible. Well, I agree with you that the crisis is one that calls for thought. I wonder if the simplest thing might not be for Bill just to fold his tent like the Arabs and silently steal away.'

'You mean leave the castle? Leave me?'

'It seems the wise move.'

'I won't have him steal away!'

'Surely it is better to steal away than a pig?'

'I'd die here without him. Can't you think of something better than that?'

'What we want is to gain time.'

'How can we? The −'

'Please!'

'The woman said she had to have his answer tomorrow.'

'As soon as that? Well, Bill will have to consent and tell her that she must give him a couple of days to nerve himself to the task.'

'What's the good of that?'

'We gain time.'

'Only two days.'

'But two days during which I shall be giving the full force of the Ickenham brain to the problem, and there are few problems capable of standing up to that treatment for long. They can't take it.'

'And when the two days are up and you haven't thought of anything?'

'Why, then,' admitted Lord Ickenham, 'the situation becomes a little sticky.'

CHAPTER SIX

I

A mong other notable observations, too numerous to mention here, the poet Dryden (1631–1700) once said that mighty things from small beginnings grow, and all thinking men are agreed that in making this statement he called his shots correctly.

If a fly had not got into his bedroom and started buzzing about his nose in the hearty way flies have, it is improbable that Lord Emsworth would have awoken on the following morning at twenty minutes to five, for he was as a rule a sound sleeper who seldom failed to enjoy his eight hours. And if he had not woken and been unable to doze off again, he would not have lain in bed musing on the Church Lads. And if he had not mused on the Church Lads, he would not have recalled Lord Ickenham's advice of the previous day. Treacherous though his memory habitually was, it all came back to him.

Sneak down to the lake in the small hours of the morning and cut the ropes of the boys' tent, Ickenham had said, and the more he examined the suggestion, the more convinced he became that this was the manly thing to do. These fellows like Ickenham, he told himself, cautious conservative men of the world, do not make snap decisions; they think things over before coming to a conclusion, and when they tell you how to act, you know that by following their instructions you will be acting for the best.

No morning hour could be smaller than the present one, and in his library, he knew, there was a paper-knife of the type with which baronets get stabbed in the back in novels of suspense, and having cut his finger on it only two days ago he had no doubts of its fitness for the purpose he had in mind. Conditions, in short, could scarcely have been more favourable.

The only thing that held him back was the thought of his sister Constance. No one knew better than he how high was her standard of behaviour for brothers, and if the pitiless light of day were to be thrown on the crime he was contemplating, she would undoubtedly extend herself. She could, he estimated, be counted on for at least ten thousand words of rebuke and recrimination, administered in daily instalments over the years. In fact, as he put it to himself, for he was given to homely phrases, he would never hear the end of it.

If Connie finds out . . . he thought, and a shudder ran through him.

Then a voice seemed to whisper in his ear.

'She won't find out,' said the voice, and he was strong again. Filled with the crusading spirit which had animated ancestors of his who had done well at the battles of Acre and Joppa, he rose from his bed and dressed, if putting on an old sweater and a pair of flannel trousers with holes in the knees could be called dressing. When he reached the library his mood was definitely that of those distant forebears who had stropped their battle-axes and sallied out to fight the Paynim.

As he left the library, brandishing the paper-knife as King Arthur had once brandished the sword Excalibur, a sudden hollowness in his interior reminded him that he had not had his morning cup of tea. Absent-minded though he was, he realized that this could be remedied by going to the kitchen. It was not a part of the castle which he ever visited these days, but as a boy he had always been in and out – in when he wanted cake and out when the cook caught him getting it, and he had no difficulty in finding his way there. Full of anticipation of the happy ending, for though he knew he had his limitations he was pretty sure that he could boil a kettle, he pushed open the familiar door and went in, and was unpleasantly surprised to see his grandson George there, eating eggs and bacon.

'Oh, hullo, Grandpa,' said George, speaking thickly, for his mouth was full.

'George!' said Lord Emsworth, also speaking thickly, but for a different reason. 'You are up very early.'

George said he liked rising betimes. You got two breakfasts that way. He was at the age when the young stomach wants all that is coming to it.

'Why are you up so early, Grandpapa?'

'I . . . er . . . I was unable to sleep.'

'Shall I fry you an egg?'

'Thank you, no. I thought of taking a little stroll. The air is so nice and fresh. Er – good-bye, George.'

'Good-bye, Grandpapa.'

'Little stroll,' said Lord Emsworth again, driving home his point, and withdrew, feeling rather shaken.

The big story of the cut tent ropes broke shortly before breakfast, when a Church Lad who looked as if he had had a disturbed night called at the back premises of the castle asking to see Beach. To him he revealed the position of affairs, and Beach dispatched an underling to find fresh rope to take the place of the severed strands. He then reported to Lady Constance, who told the Duke, who told his nephew Archie Gilpin, who told Lord Ickenham, who said, 'Well, well well! Just fancy!'

'The work of an international gang, do you think?' he said, and Archie said Well, anyway, the work of somebody who wasn't fond of Church Lads, and Lord Ickenham agreed that this might well be so.

Normally at this hour he would have been on his way to his hammock, but obviously the hammock must be postponed till later. His first task was to seek Lord Emsworth out and offer his congratulations. He was feeling quite a glow as he proceeded to the library, where he knew that the other would have retired to read *Whiffle On The Care Of The Pig* or some other volume of porcine interest, his invariable procedure after he had had breakfast. It gratified the kindly man to know that his advice had been taken with such excellent results.

Lord Emsworth was not actually reading when he entered. He was sitting staring before him, the book on his lap. There are moments when even Whiffle cannot hold the attention, and this was one of them. It would be too much, perhaps, to say that remorse gripped Lord Emsworth, but he was undoubtedly in something of a twitter and wondering if that great gesture of his had been altogether well-advised. His emotions were rather similar to those of a Chicago business man of the old school who has rubbed out a competitor with a pineapple bomb and, while feeling that that part of it is all right, cannot help speculating on what the F.B.I. are going to do when they hear about it.

'Oh – er – hullo, Ickenham,' he said. 'Nice morning.'

'For you, my dear Emsworth, a red-letter morning. I've just heard the news.'

'Eh?'

'The place is ringing with the story of your exploit.'

'Eh?'

'Now come,' said Lord Ickenham reproachfully. 'No need to dissemble with me. You took my advice, didn't you, and pulled a sword of Gideon on those tented boys? And I imagine that you are feeling a better, cleaner man.'

Lord Emsworth was looking somewhat more guilty and apprehensive than good, clean men usually do. He peered through his pince-nez at the wall, as if suspecting it of having ears.

'I wish you wouldn't talk so loudly, Ickenham.'

'I'll whisper.'

'Yes, do,' said Lord Emsworth, relieved.

Lord Ickenham took a seat and sank his voice.

'Tell me all about it.'

'Well –'

'I understand. You are a man of action, and words don't come to you easily. Like Bill Bailey.'

'Bill Bailey?'

'Fellow I know.'

'There was a song called "Won't You Come Home, Bill Bailey?" I used to sing it as a boy.'

'It must have sounded wonderful. But don't sing it now. I want to hear all about your last night's activities.'

'It was this morning.'

'Ah, yes, that was the time I recommended, wasn't it? With dawn pinking the eastern sky and the early bird chirping over its early worm. I had a feeling that you would be in better shape under those romantic conditions. You thoroughly enjoyed it, no doubt?'

'I was terrified, Ickenham.'

'Nonsense. I know you better than that.'

'I was. I kept thinking what my sister Constance would say, if she found out.'

'She won't find out.'

'You really think so?'

'How can she?'

'She does find out things.'

'But not this one. It will remain one of those great historic mysteries like the Man in the Iron Mask and the *Mary Celeste*.'

'Have you seen Constance?'

'For a moment.'

'Was she – er – upset?'

'One might almost say she split a gusset.'

'I feared as much.'

'But that's nothing for you to worry about. Your name never came up. Suspicion fell immediately on the boy who cleans the knives and boots. Do you know him?'

'No, we have never met.'

'Nice chap, I believe. Percy is his name, and apparently his relations with the Church Lads have been far from cordial. They tell me he is rather acutely alive to class distinctions and being on the castle payroll has always looked down on the

Church Lads as social inferiors. This has led to resentment, thrown stones, the calling of opprobrious names and so forth, so that when the authorities were apprised of what had happened, he automatically became the logical suspect. Taken into the squad room and grilled under the lights, however, he persisted in stout denial and ultimately had to be released for lack of evidence. That is the thing that is baffling the prosecution, the total lack of evidence.'

'I'm glad of that.'

'You ought to be.'

'But I keep thinking of Constance.'

'You're not afraid of her?'

'Yes, I am. You have no notion how she goes on about a thing. On and on and on. I remember coming down to dinner one night when we had a big dinner party with a brass paper-fastener in my shirt front, because I had unfortunately swallowed my stud, and she kept harping on it for months.'

'I see. Well, I'm sure you need have no uneasiness. Why should she suspect you?'

'She knows I have a grievance against these boys. They knocked off my top hat at the school treat and teased the Empress with a potato on a string. She may put two and two together.'

'Not a chance,' said Lord Ickenham heartily. 'I'm sure you're in the clear. But if she does start anything, imitate the intrepid Percy and stick to stout denial. You can't beat it as a general policy. Keep telling yourself that suspicion won't get her anywhere, she must have proof, and she knows perfectly well that there is none that would have a hope of getting past the Director of Public Prosecutions. If she pulls you in and wants you to make a statement, just look her in the eye and keep saying "Is zat so?" and "Sez you", confident that she can never pin the rap on you. And if she tries any funny business with a rubber hose, see your lawyer. And now I must be leaving you. I am long overdue at my hammock.'

Left alone, Lord Emsworth, though considerably cheered by these heartening words, still did not feel equal to resuming his perusal of *Whiffle On the Care Of The Pig*. He sat staring before him, and so absorbed was he in his meditations that the knock on the door brought him out of his chair, quivering in every limb.

'Come in,' he quavered, though reason told him that this could not be his sister Constance, come to ask him to make a statement, for Connie would not have knocked.

It was Lavender Briggs who entered. In her bearing, though he was too agitated to observe it, there was an unaccustomed jauntiness, a jauntiness occasioned by the fact that after dinner on the previous night the Duke had handed her a cheque for five hundred pounds and she was going to London for the night to celebrate. There are few things that so lend elasticity to a girl's step as the knowledge that in the bag swinging from her right hand there is a cheque for this sum payable to herself. Lavender Briggs was not actually skipping like the high hills, but she came within measurable distance of doing so. On her way to the library she had been humming a morceau from one of the avant-garde composers and sketching out preliminary plans for that typewriting bureau for which she now had the requisite capital.

Her prospects, she felt, were of the brightest. She could think off-hand of at least a dozen poets and as many whimsical essayists in her own circle of friends who were always writing something and having to have it typed. Shade her prices a little in the first month or so, and all these Aubreys and Lionels and Lucians and Eustaces would come running, and after them – for the news of good work soon gets around – the general public. Every red-blooded man in England, she knew, not to mention the red-blooded women, was writing a novel and would have to have top copy and two carbons.

It was consequently with something approaching cheeriness that she addressed Lord Emsworth.

'Oh, Lord Emsworth, I am sorry to disturb you, but Lady Constance has given me leave to go to London for the night. I was wondering if there was anything I could do for you while I am there?'

Lord Emsworth thanked her and said No, he could not think of anything, and she went her way, leaving him to his thoughts. He was still feeling boneless and had asked himself for the hundredth time if his friend Ickenham's advice about stout denial could be relied on to produce the happy ending, when a second knock on the door brought him out of his chair again.

This time it was Bill Bailey.

'Could I see you for a moment, Lord Emsworth?' said Bill.

3

Having interviewed Lavender Briggs and given her permission to go to London for the night, Lady Constance had retired to her boudoir to look through the letters which had arrived for her by the morning post. One of them was from her friend James Schoonmaker in New York, and she was reading it with the pleasure which his letters always gave her, when from the other side of the door there came a sound like a mighty rushing wind, and Lord Emsworth burst over the threshold. And she was about to utter a rebuking 'Oh, Clarence!', the customary formula for putting him in his place, when she caught sight of his face and the words froze on her lips.

He was a light mauve in colour, and his eyes, generally so mild, glittered behind their pince-nez with a strange light. It needed but a glance to tell her that he was in one of his rare berserk moods. These occurred perhaps twice in each calendar year, and even she, strong woman though she was, always came near to quailing before them, for on these occasions he ceased to be a human doormat whom an 'Oh, Clarence!' could quell and become something more on the order of one of those high winds which from time to time blow through the state of Kansas and send its inhabitants scurrying nimbly to their cyclone cellars. When the oppressed rise and start setting about the oppressor, their fury is always formidable. One noticed this in the French Revolution.

'Where's that damned Briggs woman?' he demanded, snapping out the words as if he had been a master of men and not a craven accustomed to curl up in a ball at the secretary's lightest glance. 'Have you seen that blasted female anywhere, Constance? I've been looking for her all over the place.'

Normally, Lady Constance would have been swift to criticize such laxity of speech, but until his belligerent mood had blown over she knew that the voice of authority must be silent.

'I let her go to London for the night,' she replied almost meekly.

'So you did,' said Lord Emsworth. He had forgotten this, as he forgot most things. 'Yes, that's right, she told me. I'm going to London, she said, yes, I remember now.'

'Why do you want Miss Briggs?'

Lord Emsworth, who had shown signs of calming down a little, returned to boiling point. His pince-nez flew off his nose and danced at the end of their string, their practice whenever he was deeply stirred.

'I'm going to sack her!'

'What!'

'She doesn't stay another day in the place. I've just been sacking Wellbeloved.'

It would be putting it too crudely to say that Lady Constance bleated, but the sound that proceeded from her did have a certain resemblance to the utterance of a high-strung sheep startled while lunching in a meadow. She was not one of George Cyril Wellbeloved's warmest admirers, but she knew how greatly her brother valued his services and she found it incredible that he should voluntarily have dispensed with them. She could as readily imagine herself dismissing Beach, that peerless butler. She shrank a little in her chair. The impression she received was that this wild-eyed man was running amok, and there shot into her mind those ominous words the Duke had spoken on the previous afternoon. 'Definitely barmy,' he had said. 'Reached the gibbering stage and may become dangerous at any moment.' It was not too fanciful to suppose that that moment had arrived.

'But, Clarence!' she cried, and Lord Emsworth, who had recovered his pince-nez, waved them at her in a menacing manner, like a retarius in the Roman arena about to throw his net.

'It's no good sitting there saying "But, Clarence!"' he said, replacing the pince-nez on his nose and glaring through them.

'I told him he'd got to be out of the place in ten minutes or I'd be after him with a shot-gun.'

'But, Clarence!'

'Don't keep saying that!'

'No, no, I'm sorry. I was only wondering why.'

Lord Emsworth considered the question. It seemed to him a fair one.

'You mean why did I sack him? I'll tell you why I sacked him. He's a snake in the grass. He and the Briggs woman were plotting to steal my pig.'

'What!'

'Are you deaf? I said they were plotting to steal the Empress.'

'But Clarence!'

'And if you say "But, Clarence!" once more, just once more,' said Lord Emsworth sternly, 'I'll know what to do about it. I suppose what you're trying to tell me is that you don't believe me.'

'How can I believe you? Miss Briggs came with the highest testimonials. She is a graduate of the London School of Economics.'

'Well, apparently the course she took there was the one on how to steal pigs.'

'But, Clarence!'

'I have warned you, Constance!'

'I'm sorry. I meant you must be mistaken.'

'Mistaken be blowed! I had the whole sordid story from the lips of Ickenham's friend Meriwether. He told it me in pitiless detail. According to him, some hidden hand wants the Empress and has bribed the Briggs woman to steal her for him. I would have suspected Sir Gregory Parsloe as the mastermind behind the plot, only he's in the South of France. Though he could have made the preliminary arrangements by letter, I suppose.'

Lady Constance clutched her temples.

'Mr Meriwether?'

'You know Meriwether. Large chap with a face like a gorilla?'

'But how could Mr Meriwether possibly have known?'

'She told him.'

'*Told* him?'

'That's right. She wanted him to be one of her corps of assistants, working with Wellbeloved. She approached him yesterday and said that if he didn't agree to help steal the Empress, she would expose him. Must have been a nasty shock to the poor fellow. Not at all the sort of thing you want to have women coming and saying to you.'

Lady Constance, who had momentarily relaxed her grip on her temples, tightened it again. She had an uneasy feeling that, unless she did so, her head would split.

'Expose him?' she whispered hoarsely. 'What do you mean?'

'What do I mean? Oh, I see. What do I mean? Yes, quite. I ought to have explained that oughtn't I? It seems that his name isn't Meriwether. It's something else which I've forgotten. Not that it matters. The point is that the Briggs woman found out somehow that he was here under an alias, as I believe the expression is, and held it over him.'

'You mean he's an imposter?'

Lady Constance spoke with a wealth of emotion. In the past few years Blandings Castle had been peculiarly rich in imposters, notable among them Lord Ickenham and his nephew Pongo, and she had reached saturation point as regarded them, never wanting to see another of them as long as she lived. A hostess gets annoyed and frets when she finds that every second guest whom she entertains is enjoying her hospitality under a false name, and it sometimes seemed to her that Blandings Castle had imposters the way other houses had mice, a circumstance at which her proud spirit rebelled.

'Who is this man?' she demanded. 'Who is he?'

'Ah, there I'm afraid you rather have me,' said Lord Emsworth. 'He told me, but you know what my memory's like. I do remember he said he was a curate.'

Lady Constance had risen from her chair and was staring at him as if instead of her elder brother he had been the Blandings Castle spectre, a knight in armour carrying his head in his hand, who was generally supposed to be around and about whenever there was going to be a death in the family. Ever since she had discovered that Myra Schoonmaker had formed an attachment to the Reverend Cuthbert Bailey, any mention of curates had affected her profoundly.

'What! What did you say?'

'When?'

'Did you say he was a curate?'

'Who?'

'Lord Ickenham's friend, Mr Meriwether.'

'Oh, ah, yes, quite, Mr Meriwether, to be sure.' Lord Emsworth's fury had expended itself, and he was now his amiable, chatty – or, as some preferred to call it, gibbering – self once more. 'Yes, he's a curate, he tells me. He doesn't look like one, but he is. That was why he refused to be a party to the purloining of my pig. Being in holy orders, his conscience wouldn't let him. I must say I thought it very civil of him to come and warn me of the Briggs woman's foul plot, knowing that it would mean her exposing him to you and you cutting up rough. But he said he had these scruples, and they wouldn't allow him to remain silent. A splendid young man, I thought, and very sound on pigs. Odd, because I didn't know they had pigs in Brazil, or curates either, for that matter. By the way, I've just remembered his name. It's Bailey. You want to keep this very clear, or you'll get muddled. He's got two names, one wrong, the other right. His wrong name's Meriwether, and his right name's Bailey.'

Lady Constance had uttered a wordless cry. She might have known, she was feeling bitterly, that Lord Ickenham would never have brought a friend to Blandings Castle unless with some sinister purpose. That much could be taken as read. But she had never suspected that even he would go to such lengths of depravity as to introduce the infamous Bailey into her home. So that, she told herself, was why Myra Schoonmaker had suddenly become so cheerful recently. Her lips tightened. Well, she was reflecting grimly, it would not be long before Blandings Castle saw the last of Lord Ickenham and his clerical friend.

'Yes, Bailey,' said Lord Emsworth. 'The Reverend Cuthbert Bailey. I was telling Ickenham just now that there was a song years ago called "Won't You Come Home, Bill Bailey?" I used to sing it as a boy. But why he should have brought the chap here under the name of Meriwether and told me he was in the Brazil-nut industry, I can't imagine. Silly kind of thing to do, wouldn't you say? I mean, if a fellow's name's Bailey, why call him Meriwether? And why say he's come from Brazil when he's come from Bottleton East? Doesn't make sense.'

'Clarence!'

'About that song,' said Lord Emsworth. 'Very catchy tune it

had. The verse escapes me – in fact, I don't believe I ever sang it – but the chorus began "Won't you come home, Bill Bailey, won't you come home?" Now, how did the next line go? Something about "the whole day long", and you had to make the "long" two syllables. "Lo-ong", if you follow me.'

'Clarence!'

'Eh?'

'Go and find Lord Ickenham.'

'Lord who?'

'Ickenham.'

'Oh, you mean Ickenham. Yes, certainly, of course, delighted. I think he usually goes and lies in that hammock on the lawn after breakfast.'

'Well, ask him if he will be good enough to leave his hammock, if it is not inconveniencing him, and come and see me immediately,' said Lady Constance.

She sank into her chair, and sat there breathing softly through the nostrils. A frozen calm had fallen on her. Her lips had tightened, her eyes were hard, and even Lord Ickenham, intrepid though he was, might have felt, had he entered at this moment, a pang of apprehension at the sight of her, so clearly was her manner that of a woman about to say to her domestic staff, 'Throw these men out, and see to it that they land on something sharp.'

CHAPTER SEVEN

I

Breakfast concluded, the Duke of Dunstable had gone to the terrace, where there was a comfortable deck-chair in the shade of a spreading tree, to smoke the first cigar of the day and read his *Times*. But scarcely had he blown the opening puff of smoke and set eye to print when his peace was destroyed by the same treble voice which had disturbed him on the previous day. Once more it squeaked in his ear, and he saw that he had been joined by Lord Emsworth's grandson George, who, as on the former occasion, had omitted to announce his presence by blowing his horn.

He did not strike the lad, for that would have involved rising from his seat, but he gave him an unpleasant look. Intrusion on his sacred after-breakfast hour always awoke the fiend that slept in him.

'Go away, boy!' he boomed.

'You mean "Scram!", don't you, chum?' said George, who liked to get these things right. 'But I want to confer with you about this tent business.'

'What tent business?'

'That thing that happened last night.'

'Oh, that?'

'Only it wasn't last night, it was this morning. A mysterious affair. Have you formed any conclusions?'

The Duke stirred irritably. He was regretting the mistaken kindness that had led him to brighten Blandings Castle with his presence. It was the old story. You said to yourself in a weak and sentimental moment that Emsworth and Connie and the rest of them led dull lives and needed cheering up by association with a polished man of the world, so you sacrificed yourself and came here, and the next thing you knew everyone was jumping into lakes and charging you five hundred pounds for stealing pigs and coming squeaking in your ear and so on and so forth – in short, making the place a ruddy inferno. He gave an animal snarl, and even when filtered through his moustache the sound was impressive, though it left George unmoved. To George it merely seemed that his old friend had got an insect of some kind in his thoracic cavity.

'What do you mean, have I formed any conclusions? Do you think a busy man like myself has time to bother himself with these trifles? Scram, boy, and let me read my paper.'

Like most small boys, George had the quiet persistence of a gadfly. It was never easy to convince him that his society was not desired by one and all. He settled himself on the stone flooring beside the Duke's chair in the manner of one who has come to stay. Limpets on rocks could have picked up useful hints from him in the way of technique.

'This is a lot hotter news than anything you'll read in the paper,' he squeaked. 'I have a strange story to relate.'

In spite of himself, the Duke found that he was becoming mildly interested.

'I suppose you know who did it, hey?' he said satirically.

George shrugged a shoulder.

'Beyond the obvious facts that the miscreant was a Freemason, left-handed, chewed tobacco and had travelled in the east,' he said, 'I have so far formed no conclusion.'

'What on earth are you talking about?'

'I only put that in to make it sound better. As a matter of fact, it was Grandpapa.'

'What do you mean, it was Grandpapa? Who was Grandpapa?'

'The miscreant.'

'Are you telling me that your grandfather –'

Words failed the Duke. His opinion of Lord Emsworth's I.Q. was, as we know, low, but he was unable to credit him with the supreme pottiness necessary for the perpetration of an act like the one they were discussing. Then, thinking again, he felt that there might be something in what the boy said. After all, from making an exhibition of oneself by maundering over a pig to sneaking out at daybreak and cutting tent ropes is but a step.

'What makes you think that?' he said, now definitely agog.

George would have liked to say, 'You know my methods. Apply them,' but it would have wasted time, and he was anxious to get on with his story.

'Shall I tell it you from the beginning, omitting no detail, however slight?'

'Certainly, certainly,' said the Duke, and would have added, 'I am all ears,' if the expression had been familiar to him. He wished the boy had a voice in a rather lower register, but in consideration of the importance of what he had to communicate he was willing to be squeaked at.

George marshalled his thoughts.

'I was in the kitchen at five o'clock this morning –'

'What were you doing there at such an hour?'

'Oh, just looking around,' said George guardedly. He knew that there was a school of thought that disapproved of these double breakfasts of his, and nothing to be gained by imparting information which might be relayed to Lady Constance, the head of that school. 'I sort of happened to go in.'

'Well?'

'And I hadn't been there more than about a couple of ticks when Grandpapa entered. He had a knife on his person.'

'A knife?'

'A whacking great scimitar.'

'How do you mean, on his person?'

'Well, actually he was brandishing it. His manner was strange, and there was a wild glitter in his eyes. So I said to myself, "Ho!"'

'You said what?'

'Ho!'

'Why "Ho!"'

'Well, wouldn't you have said "Ho!"?'

The Duke considered the question, and saw that the lad had a point there.

'No doubt I should have been surprised,' he admitted.

'So was I. That's why I said "Ho!"'

'To yourself?'

'Of course. You can't go about saying "Ho!" to people out loud. So when he went out, I followed him.'

'Why?'

'Use your loaf, big boy,' pleaded George. 'You know my methods. Apply them,' he said, happy to get it in at last. 'I wanted to see what he was up to.'

'Of course. Yes, quite understandable. And –?'

'He headed for the lake. I trickled after him, taking advantage of every inch of cover, and he made a beeline for that tent and started sawing away at the ropes.'

A sudden suspicion darted into the Duke's mind. He puffed a menacing moustache.

'If this is some silly joke of yours, young man –'

'I swear it isn't. I tell you I was watching him the whole time. He didn't see me because I was well concealed behind a neighbouring bush, but I was an eye-witness throughout. Did you ever read *The Hound of the Baskervilles*?'

For an instant the Duke received the impression that the pottiness of Lord Emsworth had been inherited by his grandson, with an assist from the latter's father, the ninth Earl's elder son, Lord Bosham, whom he knew to be one of England's less bright minds. You don't, he reasoned, read hounds, you gallop after them on horses, shouting "Yoicks!" or possibly "Tally-ho!" Then it occurred to him that the lad might be referring to some book or other. He inquired whether this was so, and received an answer in the affirmative.

'I was thinking of the bit where Holmes and Watson are lurking in the mist, waiting for the bad guy to start things moving. It was rather like that, only there wasn't any mist.'

'So you saw him clearly?'

'With the naked eye.'

'And he was cutting the ropes?'

'With the naked knife.'

The Duke relapsed into a gloomy silence. Like many another thinker before him, he was depressed by the reflection that nothing ever goes just right in this fat-headed world.

Always there is the fatal snag in the path that pulls you up sharp when the happy ending seems in sight.

A man of liberal views, he had no objection whatsoever to a little gentlemanly blackmail, and here, you would have said, the luck of the Dunstables had handed him the most admirable opportunity for such blackmail. All he had to do was to go to Lord Emsworth, tell him that his sins had found him out, demand the Empress as the price of his silence, and the wretched man would have no option but to meet his terms. The thing was a walkover. In the bag, as he believed the expression was nowadays.

Such had been his thoughts as he listened to the boy's story, but now despondency had set in. The whole project, he saw, became null and void because of one small snag – that proof of the crime depended solely on the unsupported word of the witness George. If Emsworth, as he was bound to do, pleaded not guilty to the charge, who was going to believe the testimony of a child with ginger hair and freckles, whose reputation as a teller of truth had never been one to invite scrutiny? His evidence would be laughed out of court, and he would be dashed lucky if he were not sent to bed without his supper and deprived of his pocket money for months and months.

Engrossed in these sombre thoughts, he was only dimly aware that the squeaky voice was continuing to squeak. It seemed to be saying something about motion pictures, a subject in which he had never taken even a tepid interest.

'Shut up, boy, and pop off,' he grunted.

'But I thought you'd like to know,' said George, pained.

'If you think I want to hear about a lot of greasy actors grinning on a screen, you are very much mistaken.'

'But this wasn't a greasy, grinning actor, it was Grandpapa.'

'What's that?'

'I was telling you I took pictures of Grandpapa with my camera.'

The Duke quivered as if he had been the sea monster he rather closely resembled and a harpoon had penetrated his skin.

'In the act of cutting those ropes?' he gasped.

'That's right. I've got the film upstairs in my room. I was going to take it into Market Blandings this afternoon to have it developed.'

The Duke quivered again, his emotion such that he could scarcely speak.

'You must do nothing of the sort. And you must not say a word of this to anyone.'

'Well, of course, I won't. I only told you because I thought you'd think it was funny.'

'It is very far from funny. It is extremely serious. Do you realize what would happen when the man developed that film, as you call it, and recognized your grandfather?'

'Coo! I never thought of that. You mean he'd blow the gaff? Spread the story hither and thither? Squeal on him?'

'Exactly. And your grandfather's name in the county would be –'

'Mud?'

'Precisely. Everyone would think he was potty.'

'He *is* rather potty.'

'Not so potty as he would seem if that film were made public. Dash it, they'd certify him without blinking an eye.'

'Who would?'

'The doctors, of course.'

'You mean he'd be put in a loony bin?'

'Exactly.'

'Coo!'

George could see now why his companion had said it was serious. He was very fond of Lord Emsworth, and would have hated to find him winding up in a padded cell. He felt in his pocket and produced a bag of acid drops, always a great help to thought. Chewing one of these, he sat pondering in silence. The Duke resumed his remarks.

'Do you understand what I am saying?'

George nodded.

'I dig you, Chief.'

'Don't say "I dig you" and don't call me "chief". Bring the thing to me, and I'll take care of it. It's not safe in the hands of a mere child like you.'

'Okay, big boy.'

'And don't call me big boy,' said the Duke.

2

There was a contented smile on Lord Ickenham's face as he settled himself in his hammock after leaving Lord Emsworth. It gratified him to feel that he had allayed the latter's fears and eased his mind. Nothing like a pep talk, he was thinking, and he was deep in a pleasant reverie when a voice spoke his name and he perceived Lord Emsworth at his side, drooping like a tired lily. Except when he had something to prop himself against, there was always a suggestion of the drooping floweret about the master of Blandings Castle. He seemed to work on a hinge somewhere in the small of his back, and people searching for something nice to say of him sometimes described him as having a scholarly stoop. Lord Ickenham had become accustomed to this bonelessness and no longer expected his friend to give any evidence of possessing vertebrae, but the look of anguish on his face was new, and it shocked him. He rose from the hammock with lissom leap, full of sympathy and concern.

'Good heavens, Emsworth! What's the matter? Is something wrong?'

For some moments it seemed as though speech would prove beyond the ninth earl's powers and that he would continue indefinitely to give his rather vivid impersonation of a paralysed deaf mute. But eventually he spoke.

'I've just seen Dunstable,' he said.

Lord Ickenham remained perplexed. The situation did not appear to him to have been clarified. He, personally, would always prefer not to see the Duke, a preference shared by the latter's many acquaintances in Wiltshire and elsewhere, but it did not disturb him unduly when he had to, and he found it strange that his companion should be of less stern stuff.

'Unavoidable, don't you think when he's staying in the house?' he said. 'There he is, I mean to say, and you can't very well help running into him from time to time. But perhaps he said something to upset you?'

The anguished look in Lord Emsworth's eyes became more anguished. It was as if the question had touched an exposed nerve. He gulped for a moment, reminding Lord Ickenham of a dog to which he was greatly attached, which made a similar sound when about to give up its all after a too busy day among the fleshpots.

'He said he wanted the Empress.'

'Who wouldn't?'

'And I've got to give her to him.'

'You've *what*?'

'The alternative was too terrible to contemplate. He threatened, if I refused, to tell Constance that it was I who cut those tent ropes.'

Lord Ickenham began to feel a little impatient. He had already told this man, in words adapted to the meanest intelligence, what course to pursue, should suspicion fall upon him.

'My dear fellow, don't you remember what I said to you in the library? Stick to stout denial.'

'But he has proof.'

'Proof?'

'Eh? Yes, proof. It seems that my grandson George took photographs of me with his camera, and Dunstable now has the film in his possession. And I gave George that camera for his birthday! "This will keep you out of mischief, George, my boy," I remember saying. Out of mischief!' said Lord Emsworth bitterly, his air that of a grandfather regretting that he had ever been so foolish as to beget a son who in his turn would beget a son of his own capable of using a camera. There were, he was feeling, far too many grandsons in the world and far too many cameras for them to take pictures of grandfathers with. His view of grandsons was, in short, at the moment jaundiced, and as, having told his tale, he moved limply away, he was thinking almost as harshly of George as of the Duke of Dunstable.

Lord Ickenham returned to his hammock. He always thought more nimbly when in a recumbent position, and it was plain to him that a considerable amount of nimble thinking was now called for. Hitherto, his endeavours to spread sweetness and light and give service with a smile had been uniformly successful, but a man whose aim in life it is to do the square thing by his fellows is never content to think with modest pride of past triumphs; it is the present on which he feels the mind must be fixed, and it was to Lord Emsworth's problem that he gave the full force of his powerful intellect.

It was a problem which undoubtedly presented certain points of interest, and at the moment he confessed himself unable to see how it was to be solved. Given the unhappy man's panic fear of having Lady Constance's attention drawn to his recent activities, there seemed no course for Lord Emsworth to pursue but to meet the Duke's terms. It was one of those occasions, more frequent in real life than on the television and motion picture screens, when the bad guy comes out on top and the good guy gets the loser's end. The Duke of Dunstable might not look like a green bay tree, but everything pointed to the probability of him flourishing like one.

He was musing thus, and had closed his eyes in order to muse the better, when a stately figure approached the hammock and stood beside it. Shrewdly realizing that there was but the slimmest chance of her brother Clarence remembering to tell Lord Ickenham that his presence was desired in her boudoir, Lady Constance had rung for Beach and sent him off to act as a substitute messenger. The butler coughed respectfully, and Lord Ickenham opened his eyes.

'Pardon me for disturbing you, m'lord –'

'Not at all, Beach, not at all,' said Lord Ickenham heartily. He was always glad to chat with this pillar of Blandings, for a firm friendship had sprung up between them during his previous sojourn at the castle, and this second visit had cemented it. 'Something on your mind?'

'Her ladyship, m'lord.'

'What about her?'

'If it is convenient to you m'lord, she would be glad to see you for a moment in her boudoir.'

This struck Lord Ickenham as unusual. It was the first time his hostess had gone out of her way to seek his company, and he was not sure that he liked the look of things. He had never considered himself psychic, but he was conscious of a strong premonition that trouble was about to raise its ugly head.

'Any idea what she wants?'

Butlers rarely display emotion, and there was nothing in Beach's manner to reveal the sympathy he was feeling for one who, in his opinion, was about to face an ordeal somewhat comparable to that of the prophet Daniel when he entered the lions' den.

'I rather fancy, m'lord, her ladyship wishes to confer with you on the subject of Mr Meriwether. With reference to the gentleman's name being in reality the Reverend Cuthbert Bailey.'

Once in his cowboy days Lord Ickenham, injudiciously standing behind a temperamental mule, had been kicked by the animal in the stomach. He felt now rather as he had felt then, though only an involuntary start showed that he was not his usual debonair self.

'Oh,' he said thoughtfully. 'Oh. So she knows about that?'

'Yes, m'lord.'

'How did you come to get abreast?'

'I was inadvertently an auditor of his lordship's conversation with her ladyship. I chanced to be passing the door, and his lordship had omitted to close it.'

'And you stopped, looked and listened?'

'I had paused to tie my shoelace,' said Beach with dignity. 'I found it impossible not to overhear what his lordship was saying.'

'And what was he saying?'

'He was informing her ladyship that Miss Briggs, having discovered Mr Meriwether's identity, was seeking to compel the gentleman to assist her in her project of stealing his lordship's pig, but that Mr Meriwether refused to be a party to the undertaking, having scruples. It was in the course of his remarks on this subject that his lordship revealed that Mr Meriwether was not Mr Meriwether, but Mr Bailey.'

Lord Ickenham sighed. In principle he approved of his young friend's rigid code of ethics, but there was no denying that that high-mindedness of his could be inconvenient, lowering as it did his efficiency as a plotter. The ideal person with whom to plot is the furtive, shifty-eyed man who stifled his conscience at the age of six and would not recognize a scruple if you served it up to him on an individual blue plate with béarnaise sauce.

'I see,' he said. 'How did Lady Constance take this piece of hot news?'

'She appeared somewhat stirred, m'lord.'

'One sees how she might well be. And now she wants to have a word with me?'

'Yes, m'lord.'

'To thresh the thing out, no doubt, and consider it from every angle. Oh, what a tangled web we weave, Beach, when first we practise to deceive.'

'We do, indeed, m'lord.'

'Well, all right,' said Lord Ickenham, rising. 'I can give her five minutes.'

The time it had taken Beach to deliver his message and Lord Ickenham to make the journey between lawn and boudoir was perhaps ten minutes, and with each of those minutes Lady Constance's wrath had touched a new high. At the moment when her guest entered the room she had just been thinking how agreeable it would be to skin him with a blunt knife, and the genial smile he gave her as he came in seemed to go through her nervous system like a red-hot bullet through butter. 'My tablets – Meet it is I set it down that one may smile and smile and be a villain. At least, I'm sure it may be so in Blandings Castle,' she was saying to herself.

'Beach says you want to see me, Lady Constance,' said Lord Ickenham, smiling another affectionate smile. His manner was that of a man looking forward to a delightful chat on this and that with an attractive woman, and Lady Constance, meeting the smile head on, realized that in entertaining the idea of skinning him with a blunt knife she had been too lenient. Not a blunt knife, she was thinking, but some such instrument as the one described by the poet Gilbert as looking far less like a hatchet than a dissipated saw.

'Please sit down,' she said coldly.

'Oh, thanks,' said Lord Ickenham doing so. His eye fell on a photograph on the desk. 'Hullo, this face seems familiar. Jimmy Schoonmaker?'

'Yes.'

'Taken recently?'

'Yes.'

'He looks older than he used to. One does, of course, as the years go on. I suppose I do, too, though I've never noticed it. Great chap, Jimmy. Did you know that he brought young Myra up all by himself after his wife died? With a certain amount of assistance from me. The one thing he jibbed at was giving her her bath, so he used to call me in of an evening, and I would soap her back, keeping what the advertisements call a safe suds level. It was a little like massaging an eel. Bless my soul, how long ago it seems. I remember once –'

'Lord Ickenham!' Lady Constance's voice, several degrees below zero at the outset, had become even more like that of a snow queen. The hatchet that looked like a dissipated saw would not have seemed to her barely adequate. 'I did not ask you to come here because I wished to hear your reminiscences. It was to tell you that you will leave the castle immediately. *With*,' added Lady Constance, speaking from between clenched teeth, 'your friend Mr Bailey.'

She paused, and was conscious of a feeling of flatness and disappointment. She had expected her words to bathe this man in confusion and shatter his composure to fragments, but he had not turned a hair of his neatly brushed head. He was looking at another photograph. It was that of Lady Constance's late husband, Joseph Keeble, but she gave him no time to ask questions about it.

'Lord Ickenham!'

He turned, full of apology.

'I'm sorry. I'm afraid I let my attention wander. I was thinking of the dear old days. You were saying that you were about to leave the castle, were you not?'

'I was saying that *you* were about to leave the castle.'

Lord Ickenham seemed surprised.

'I had made no plans. You're sure you mean me?'

'And you will take Mr Bailey with you. How dare you bring that impossible young man here?'

Lord Ickenham fingered his moustache thoughtfully.

'Oh, Bill Bailey. I see what you mean. Yes, I suppose it was a social solecism. But reflect. I meant well. Two young hearts had been sundered in springtime . . . well, not in springtime, perhaps, but as near to it as makes no matter, and I wanted to adjust things. I'm sure Jimmy would have approved of the kindly act.'

'I disagree with you.'

'He wants his ewe lamb to be happy.'

'So do I. That is why I do not intend to allow her to marry a penniless curate. But there is no need to discuss it. There are –'

'You'll be sorry when Bill suddenly becomes a bishop.'

'– good trains –'

'Why did I not push this good thing along, you'll say to yourself.'

'– throughout the day. I recommend the 2.15,' said Lady Constance. 'Good morning, Lord Ickenham. I will not keep you any longer.'

A nicer-minded man would have detected in these words a hint – guarded, perhaps, but nevertheless a hint – that his presence was no longer desired, but Lord Ickenham remained glued to his chair. He was looking troubled.

'I agree that you are probably right in giving this plug to the 2.15 train,' he said. 'No doubt it is an excellent one. But there are difficulties in the way of Bill and me catching it.'

'I see none.'

'I will try to make myself clearer. Have you studied Bill Bailey at all closely during his visit here? He's an odd chap.

Wouldn't hurt a fly in the ordinary way, in fact I've known him not to do so –'

'I am not interested in Mr –'

'But, when driven to it, ruthless and sticking at nothing. You might think that, being a curate, he would suppress those photographs, and of course I feel that that is what he ought to do. But even curates can be pushed too far, and I'm afraid if you insist on him leaving the castle, however luxurious the 2.15 train, that that is how he will feel he is being pushed.'

'Lord Ickenham!'

'You spoke?'

'*What* are you talking about?'

'Didn't I explain that? I'm sorry. I have an annoying habit of getting ahead of my story. I was alluding to the photographs he took of Beach and saying that, if driven out into the snow, he will feel so bitter that he will give them wide publicity. Vindictive, yes, and not at all the sort of thing one approves of in a clerk in holy orders, but that is what will happen, I assure you.'

Lady Constance placed a hand on a forehead which had become fevered. Not even when conversing with her brother Clarence had she ever felt so marked a swimming sensation.

'Photographs? Of Beach?'

'Cutting those tent ropes and causing alarm and despondency to more Church Lads than one likes to contemplate. But how foolish of me. I didn't tell you, did I? Here is the thing in a nutshell. Bill Bailey, unable to sleep this morning possibly because love affects him that way, started to go for a stroll, saw young George's camera lying in the hall, picked it up with a vague idea of photographing some of the local fauna and was surprised to see Beach down by the lake, cutting those ropes. He took a whole reel of him and I understand they have come out splendidly. May I smoke?' said Lord Ickenham, taking out his case.

Lady Constance did not reply. She seemed to have been turned into a pillar of salt, like Lot's wife. It might have been supposed that, having passed her whole life at Blandings Castle, with the sort of things happening that happened daily in that stately but always somewhat hectic home of England, she would have been impervious to shocks. Nothing, one would have said, would have been able to surprise her. This was not so. She was stunned.

Beach! Eighteen years of spotless buttling, and now this! If she had not been seated, she would have reeled. Everything seemed to her to go black, including Lord Ickenham. He might have been an actor, made up to play Othello, lighting an inky cigarette with a sepia lighter.

'Of course,' this negroid man went on, 'one gets the thought behind Beach's rash act. For days Emsworth has been preaching a holy war against these Church Lads, filling the listening air with the tale of what he has suffered at their hands, and it is easy to understand how Beach, feudally devoted to him, felt that he could hold himself back no longer. Out with the knife and go to it, he said to himself. It will probably have occurred to you how closely in its essentials the whole set-up resembles the murder of the late St Thomas à Becket. King Henry, you will remember, kept saying, "Will no one rid me of this turbulent priest?" till those knights of his decided that something had to be done about it. Emsworth, perhaps in other words, expressed the same view about the Church Lads, and Beach, taking his duties as a butler very seriously, thought that it was part of them to show the young thugs that crime does not pay and that retribution must sooner or later overtake those who knock top hats off with crusty rolls at school treats.'

Lord Ickenham paused to cough, for he had swallowed a mouthful of smoke the wrong way. Lady Constance remained congealed. She might have been a statue of herself commissioned by a group of friends and admirers.

'You see how extremely awkward the situation is? Whether or not Emsworth formally instructed Beach to take the law into his hands, we shall probably never know, but it makes very little difference. If those photographs are given to the world, it is inevitable that Beach, unable to bear the shame of exposure, will hand in his portfolio and resign office, and you will lose the finest butler in Shropshire. And there is another thing. Emsworth will unquestionably confess that he inflamed the man and so was directly responsible for what happened, and one can see the County looking very askance at him, pursing their lips, raising their eyebrows, possibly even cutting him at the next Agricultural Show. Really, Lady Constance, if I were you, I think I would reconsider this idea of yours of giving Bill Bailey the old heave-ho. I will leave the castle on the 2.15, if you wish, though sorry to go, for I like the society here, but Bailey, I'm afraid, must stay. Possibly in the course of time his winning personality will overcome your present prejudice against him. I'll leave you to think it over,' said Lord Ickenham, and with another of his kindly smiles left the room.

For an appreciable time after he had gone Lady Constance sat motionless. Then, as if a sudden light had shone on her darkness, she gave a start. She stretched out a hand towards the pigeonholes on the desk, in which reposed notepaper, envelopes, postcards, telegraph forms and cable forms.

Selecting one of the last named, she took pen in hand, and began to write.

James Schoonmaker
1000 Park Avenue
New York

She paused a moment in thought. Then she began to write again:

'*Come immediately. Most urgent. Must see you . . .*'

4

It is always unpleasant for a man of good will to be compelled, even from the best of motives, to blacken the name of an innocent butler, and his first thought after he has done so is to make amends. Immediately after leaving Lady Constance, therefore, Lord Ickenham proceeded to Beach's pantry, where with a few well-chosen words he slipped a remorseful five-pound note into the other's hand. Beach trousered the money with a stately bow of thanks, and in answer to a query as to whether he had any knowledge of the Reverend Cuthbert Bailey's whereabouts said that he had seen him some little time ago entering the rose garden in company with Miss Schoonmaker.

Thither Lord Ickenham decided to make his way. He was sufficiently a student of human nature to be aware that, when two lovers get together in a rose garden, they do not watch the clock, and he presumed that, if Bill and Myra had been there some little time ago, they would be there now. They would, he supposed, be discussing in gloomy mood the former's imminent departure from Blandings Castle, and he was anxious to relieve their minds. For there was no doubt in his own that Lady Constance, having thought things over, would continue to extend her hospitality to the young cleric. Her whole air, as he left her, had been that of a woman unable to see any alternative to the hoisting of the white flag.

He had scarcely left the house when he saw that he had been mistaken. So far from being in the rose garden, Myra Schoonmaker was on the gravel strip outside the front door, and so far from being in conference with Bill, she was closeted, as far as one can be closeted in the open air, with the Duke of Dunstable's nephew, Archie Gilpin. As he appeared, Archie Gilpin moved away, and as Myra came towards him, he saw that her face was sombre and her walk the walk of a girl who can detect no silver lining in the clouds. This did not cause him concern. He had that to tell which would be a verbal shot in the arm and set her dancing all over the place and strewing roses from her hat.

'Hullo there,' he said.

'Oh, hullo, Uncle Fred.'

'You look pretty much down among the wines and spirits, young Myra.'

'That's the way I feel.'

'You won't much longer. Where's Bill?'

The girl shrugged her shoulders.

'Oh, somewhere around, I suppose. I left him in the rose garden.'

Lord Ickenham's eyebrows shot up.

'You *left* him in the rose garden? Not a lovers' tiff, I hope?'

'If you like to call it that,' said Myra. She kicked moodily at a passing beetle, which gave her a cold look and went on its way. 'I've broken our engagement.'

It was never easy to disconcert Lord Ickenham, as his

nephew Pongo would have testified. Even on that day at the dog races his demeanour, even after the hand of the Law had fallen on his shoulder, had remained unruffled. But now he could not hide his dismay. He looked at the girl incredulously.

'You've broken the engagement?'

'Yes.'

'But why?'

'Because he doesn't love me.'

'What makes you think that?'

'I'll tell you what makes me think that,' said Myra passionately. 'He went and told Lord Emsworth who he was, knowing that Lord Emsworth was bound to spill the beans to Lady Constance, and that Lady Constance would instantly bounce him. And why did he do it, you ask? Because it gave him the excuse to get away from me. I suppose he's got another girl in Bottleton East.'

Lord Ickenham twirled his moustache sternly. He had often in the course of his life listened patiently to people talking through their hats, but he was in no mood to be patient now.

'Myra,' he said. 'You ought to have your head examined.'

'Oh, yes?'

'It would be money well spent. I assure you that if all the girls in Bottleton East came and did the dance of the seven veils before him, Bill Bailey wouldn't give them a glance. He told Emsworth who he was because his conscience wouldn't let him do otherwise. The revelation was unavoidable if he was to make his story of the Briggs' foul plot convincing, and he did not count the cost. He knew that it meant ruin and disaster, but he refused to stand silently by and allow that good man to be deprived of his pig. You ought to be fawning on him for his iron integrity, instead of going about the place breaking engagements. I have always held that the man of sensibility should be careful what he says to the other sex, if he wishes to be numbered among the preux chevaliers, but I cannot restrain myself from telling you, young M. Schoonmaker, that you have behaved like a little half-wit.'

Myra, who had been staring at the beetle as if contemplating having another go at it, raised a startled head.

'Do you think that was really it?'

'Of course it was.'

'And he wasn't just jumping at the chance of getting away from me?'

'Of course he wasn't. I tell you, Bill Bailey is about as near being a stainless knight as you could find in a month of Sundays. He's as spotless as they come.'

A deep sigh escaped Myra Schoonmaker. His eloquence had convinced her.

'Half-wit,' she said, 'is right. Uncle Fred, I've made a ghastly fool of myself.'

'Just what I've been telling you.'

'I don't mean about Bill. I could have put that right in a minute. But I've just told Archie Gilpin I'll marry him.'

'No harm that I can see in confiding your matrimonial plans to Archie Gilpin. He'll probably send you a wedding present.'

'Oh, don't be so dumb, Uncle Fred! I mean I've just told Archie, I'll marry *him*!'

'What, *him*?'

'Yes, *him*.'

'Well, fry me for an oyster! Why on earth did you do that?'

'Oh, just a sort of gesture, I suppose. It's what they used to write in my reports at Miss Spence's school. "She is often too impulsive", they used to say.'

She spoke despondently. Ever since that brief but fateful conversation with Archie, an uneasy conviction had been stealing over her that in a rash moment she had started something which she would have given much to stop. Her emotions were somewhat similar to those of a nervous passenger on a roller coaster at an amusement park who when it is too late to get off feels the contraption gathering speed beneath him.

It was not as if she even liked Archie Gilpin very much. He was all right in his way, a pleasant enough companion for a stroll or a game of tennis, but until this awful thing had happened he had been something completely negligible, just some sort of foreign substance that happened to be around. And now she was engaged to him, and the announcement would be in *The Times*, and Lady Constance would be telling her how pleased her father would be and how sensible it was of her to have realized that that other thing had been nothing but a ridiculous infatuation, and she could see no point in going on living. She was very much inclined to go down to the lake and ask one of the Church Lads if he would care to earn a shilling by holding her head under water till the vital spark expired.

'Oh, Uncle Fred!' she said.

'There, there!' said Lord Ickenham.

'Oh, Uncle Fred!'

'Don't talk, just cry. There is nothing more therapeutic.'

'What shall I do?'

'Break it off, of course. What else? Tell him it's been nice knowing him, and hand him his hat.'

'But I can't.'

'Nonsense. Perfectly easy thing to bring into the

conversation. You're strolling with him in the moonlight. He says something about how jolly it's going to be when you and he are settled down in your little nest, and you say, "Oh, I forgot to tell you about that. It's off." He says, "What!" You say, "You heard," and he reddens and goes to Africa.'

'And I go to New York.'

'Why New York?'

'Because that's where I'll be shipped back to in disgrace when they hear I've broken my engagement to a Duke's nephew.'

'Don't tell me Jimmy's a stern father?'

'That would make him stern enough. He's got a thing about the British aristocracy. He admires them terrifically.'

'I don't blame him. We're the salt of the earth.'

'He would insist on taking me home, and I'd never see my angel Bill again, because he couldn't possibly afford the fare to New York.'

Lord Ickenham mused. This was a complication he had not taken into his calculations.

'I see. Yes, I appreciate the difficulty.'

'Me, too.'

'This opens up a new line of thought. You'd better leave everything to me.'

'I don't see that you can do anything.'

'That is always a rash observation to make to an Ickenham. As I once remarked to another young friend of mine, this sort of situation brings out the best in me. And when you get the best in Frederick Altamont Cornwallis Twistleton, fifth Earl of good old Ickenham, you've got something.'

CHAPTER EIGHT

I

If you go down Fleet Street and turn into one of the side streets leading to the river, you will find yourself confronted by a vast building that looks something like a county jail and something like a biscuit factory. This is Tilbury House, the home of the Mammoth Publishing Company, that busy hive where hordes of workers toil day and night, churning out reading matter for the masses. For Lord Tilbury's numerous daily and weekly papers are not, as is sometimes supposed, just Acts of God; they are produced deliberately.

The building has its scores of windows, but pay no attention to those on the first two floors, for there are only editors and things behind them. Concentrate the eye on the three in the middle of the third floor. These belong to Lord Tilbury's private office, and there is just a chance, if you wait, that you may catch a glimpse of him leaning out to get a breath of air, than which nothing could be more calculated to make a sightseer's day.

This morning, however, you would have been out of luck, for Lord Tilbury was sitting motionless at his desk. He had been sitting there for some little time. There were a hundred letters he should have been dictating to Millicent Rigby, his secretary, but Millicent remained in the outer office, undictated to. There were a dozen editors with whom he should have been conferring, but they stayed where they were, unconferred with.

He was deep in thought, and anyone seeing him would have asked himself with awe what it was that was occupying that giant mind. He might have been planning out some pronouncement which would shake the chancelleries, or pondering on the most suitable line to take in connexion with the latest rift in the Cabinet, or even, for he took a personal interest in all his publications, considering changes in the policy of *Wee Tots*, the journal which has done so much to mould thought in the British nursery. In actual fact, he was musing on Empress of Blandings.

In the life of every successful man there is always some little something missing. Lord Tilbury had wealth and power and the comforting knowledge that, catering as he did for readers who had all been mentally arrested at the age of twelve, he would continue to enjoy these indefinitely, but he had not got Empress of Blandings: and ever since the day when he and that ornament of her sex had met he had yearned to add her to his Buckinghamshire piggery. That was how the pig-minded always reacted to even the briefest glance at the Empress. They came, saw, gasped and went away unhappy and discontented, ever after, to move through life bemused, like men kissed by goddesses in dreams.

His sombre thoughts were broken in upon by the ringing of the telephone. Moodily he took up the receiver.

'Hoy!' shouted a voice in his ear, and he had no difficulty in identifying the speaker. He had a wide circle of acquaintances, but the Duke of Dunstable was the only member of it who opened conversations with this monosyllable in a booming tone reminiscent of a costermonger calling attention to his blood oranges. 'Is that you, Stinker?'

Lord Tilbury frowned. There were only a few survivors of the old days who addressed him thus. Even in the distant past he had found the name distasteful, and now that he had become a man of distinction, it jarred upon him even more gratingly. In addition to frowning, he also swelled a good deal. He was a short, stout man who swelled readily when annoyed.

'Lord Tilbury speaking,' he said curtly, emphasizing the first two words. 'Well?'

'What?' roared the Duke. He was a little deaf in the right ear.

'Well?'

'Speak up, Stinker. Don't mumble.'

Lord Tilbury raised his voice to an almost Duke-like pitch.

'I said "Well?".'

'Well?'

'Yes.'

'Damn silly thing to say,' said the Duke and Lord Tilbury's frown deepened.

'What is it, Dunstable?'

'Eh?'

'What *is* it?'

'What is what?'

'What do you want?' Lord Tilbury rasped, the hand gripping the receiver about to crash it back on its cradle.

'It's not what I want,' bellowed the Duke. 'It's what you want. I've got that pig.'

'What!'

'What?'

Lord Tilbury did not reply. He had stiffened in his chair and presented the appearance of somebody in a fairy story who had had a spell cast upon him by the local wizard. His silence offended the Duke, never a patient man.

'Are you there, Stinker?' he roared, and Lord Tilbury thought for a moment that his ear drum had gone.

'Yes, yes, yes,' he said, removing the receiver for a moment in order to massage his ear.

'Then why the devil don't you utter?'

'I was overcome.'

'What?'

'I could hardly believe it. You have really persuaded Emsworth to sell you Empress of Blandings?'

'We came to an arrangement. Is that offer of yours still open?'

'Of course, of course.'

'Two thousand, cash down?'

'Certainly.'

'What?'

'I said certainly.'

'Then you'd better come here and collect the animal.'

'I will. I'll –'

Lord Tilbury paused. He was thinking of all the correspondence he should have been dictating to Millicent Rigby. Could he neglect this? Then he saw the solution. He could take Millicent Rigby with him. He pressed a bell. His secretary entered.

'Where do you live, Miss Rigby?'

'Shepherd Market, Lord Tilbury.'

'Take a taxi, go and pack some things for the night, and

come back here. We're driving down to Shropshire.' He spoke into the telephone. 'Are you there, Dunstable?'

Something not unlike an explosion in an ammunition dump made itself heard at the other end of the line.

'Are *you* there, blast your gizzard? What's the matter? Can't get a word out of you.'

'I was speaking to my secretary.'

'Well, don't. Do you realize what these trunk calls cost?'

'I'm sorry. I am motoring down immediately. Where can I see you? I don't want to come to the castle.'

'Put up at the Emsworth Arms in Market Blandings. I'll meet you there.'

'I'll be waiting for you.'

'What?'

'I said I'll be waiting for you.'

'What?'

Lord Tilbury gritted his teeth. He was feeling hot and exhausted. That was the effect the other's telephone technique often had on people.

2

Lavender Briggs had caught the 12.30 train at Paddington. It set her down on the platform of Market Blandings station shortly after four.

The day was warm and the journey had been stuffy and somewhat exhausting, but her mood was one of quiet contentment. She had enjoyed every minute of her visit to the metropolis. She had deposited the Duke's cheque. She had dined with a group of earnest friends at the Crushed Pansy, the restaurant with a soul, and at the conclusion of the meal they had all gone on to the opening performance at the Flaming Youth Group Centre of one of those avant-garde plays which bring the scent of boiling cabbage across the footlights and in which the little man in the bowler hat turns out to be God. And she was confident that when she saw him the Reverend Cuthbert Bailey would have made up his mind, rather than be unmasked, to lend his services to the purloining of Lord Emsworth's pig. It seemed to her that a cup of tea was indicated by way of celebration, and she made her way to the Emsworth Arms. There were other hostelries in Market Blandings – one does not forget the Goose and Gander, the Jolly Cricketers, the Wheatsheaf, the Waggoner's Rest, the Beetle and Wedge and the Stitch in Time – but the Emsworth Arms was the only one where a lady could get a refined cup of tea with buttered toast and fancy cakes. Those other establishments catered more to the George Cyril Wellbeloved type of client and were content to say it with beer.

At the Emsworth Arms, moreover, you could have your refreshment served to you in the large garden which was one of the features of Market Blandings. Dotted about with rustic tables, it ran all the way down to the river, and there were few of the rustic tables that did not enjoy the shade of a spreading tree or a clump of bushes. The one Lavender Briggs selected was screened from view by a green mass of foliage, and she had chosen it because she wanted complete privacy in which to meditate on the very satisfactory state of her affairs. Elsewhere in the garden one's thoughts were apt to be interrupted by family groups presided over by flushed mothers telling Wilfred to stop teasing Katie or Percival to leave off making faces at Jane.

She had finished the cakes and the buttered toast and was sipping her third cup of tea, when from the other side of the bushes, where she had noticed a rustic table similar to her own, a voice spoke. All it said was 'Two beers', but at the sound of it she stiffened in her chair, some sixth sense telling her that if she listened, she might hear something of interest. For it was the Duke's voice that had shattered the afternoon stillness, and there was only one thing that could have brought the Duke to Market Blandings, the desire for a conference with the mystery man who was prepared to go as high as two thousand pounds to acquire Lord Emsworth's peerless pig.

A moment later a second voice spoke, and if Lavender Briggs had stiffened before, she stiffened doubly now. The words it had said were negligible, something about the warmth of the day, but they were enough to enable her to recognize the speaker as her former employer, Lord Tilbury of the Mammoth Publishing Company. She had taken too much dictation from those august lips in the past to allow of any misconception.

Rigid in her chair, she set herself to listen with, in the Duke's powerful phrase, her ears sticking up.

3

Conversation on the other side of the bushes was for awhile desultory. With a waiter expected back at any moment with beer, two men who have serious matters to discuss do not immediately plumb the deeps, but confine themselves to small talk. Lord Tilbury said once more that the day was warm, and the Duke agreed. The Duke said he supposed it had been even warmer in London, and Lord Tilbury said Yes, much warmer. The Duke said it wasn't the heat he minded so much as the humidity, and Lord Tilbury confessed that it was the humidity that troubled him also. Then the beer arrived, and the Duke flung himself on it with a grunt. He must have abandoned rather noticeably the gentlemanly restraint which one likes to see in Dukes when drinking beer, for Lord Tilbury said:

'You seem thirsty. Did you walk from the castle?'

'No, got a lift. Bit of luck. It's a warm day.'

'Yes, very warm.'

'Humid, too.'

'Very humid.'

'It's the humidity I don't like.'

'I don't like the humidity either.'

Silence followed these intellectual exchanges. It was broken by a loud chuckle from the Duke.

'Eh?' said Lord Tilbury.

'What?' said the Duke. 'Speak up, Stinker.'

'I was merely wondering what it was that was amusing you,' said Lord Tilbury frostily. 'And I wish you wouldn't call me Stinker. Somebody might hear.'

'Let them.'

'What the devil are you giggling about?' demanded Lord Tilbury, as a second chuckle followed the first. He had never been fond of the Duke of Dunstable, and he felt that having to put up with his society, after a fatiguing journey from London, was a heavy price to pay even for Empress of Blandings.

The Duke was not a man who made a practice of disclosing his private affairs to every dashed Tom, Dick and Harry, and at another time and under different conditions would have been blowed if he was going to let himself be pumped by Stinker Pyke, or Lord Tilbury, as he now called himself. He mistrusted these newspaper fellers. You told them something in the strictest confidence, and the next thing you knew it was spread all over the gossip page with a six-inch headline at the top and probably a photograph of you, looking like someone the police were anxious to question in connexion with the Dover Street smash-and-grab raid.

But he was now fairly full of the Emsworth Arms beer, and, as everybody who has tried it knows, there is something about the home-brewed beer purveyed by G. Ovens, landlord of the Emsworth Arms, that has a mellowing effect. What G. Ovens put into it is a secret between him and his Maker, but it acts like magic on the most reticent. With a pint of this elixir sloshing about inside him, it seemed to the Duke that it would be churlish not to share his happiness with a sympathetic crony.

'Just put one over on a blasted female,' he said.

'Lady Constance?' said Lord Tilbury, jumping to what suggested itself to him as the obvious conclusion. His visit to Blandings Castle had been a brief one, but it had enabled him to become well acquainted with his hostess.

'No, not Connie. Connie's all right. Potty, but a good enough soul. This was Emsworth's secretary, a frightful woman of the ghastly name of Briggs. Lavender Briggs,' said the Duke, as if that made it worse.

Something stirred at the back of Lord Tilbury's mind.

'Lavender Briggs? I had a secretary named Briggs, and I seem to have a recollection of hearing someone address her as Lavender.'

'Beastly name.'

'And quite unsuited to a woman of her appearance, if it's the same woman. Is she tall and ungainly?'

'Very.'

'With harlequin glasses?'

'If that's what you call them.'

'Large feet?'

'Enormous.'

'Hair like seaweed?'

'Just like seaweed. And talks rot all the time about dusty answers.'

'I never heard her do that, but from your description it must be the same woman. I sacked her.'

'You couldn't have done better.'

'She had a way of looking at me as if I were some kind of worm, and I frequently caught her sniffing. Well, I wasn't going to put up with that sort of thing. She was an excellent secretary as far as her work was concerned, but I told her she had to go. So she is with Emsworth now? He has my sympathy. But you were saying that you had – ah – put one over on her. How was that?'

'It's a long story. She tried to get five hundred pounds out of me.'

Lord Tilbury seemed for a moment bewildered. Then he understood. He was a quick-witted man.

'Breach of promise, eh? Odd that you should have been attracted by a hideous woman like Lavender Briggs. Her glasses alone, one would have thought . . . However, there is no accounting for these sudden infatuations, though one would have expected a man of your age to have had more sense. No fool like an old fool, as they say. Well, if she could prove this breach of promise – had letters and so forth – I think you got off cheap, and it should be a valuable lesson to you.'

There is just this one thing more to be said about G. Ovens' home-brewed beer. If you want to preserve that mellow fondness for all mankind which it imparts, you have to go on drinking it. The Duke, having had only a single pint, was unable to retain the feeling that Lord Tilbury was a staunch friend from whom he could have no secrets. He was conscious of a vivid dislike for him, and couldn't imagine why a gracious sovereign had bestowed a barony on a man like that. Lavender Briggs, leaning forward, alert not to miss a word, nearly fell out of her chair, so loud was the snort that rang through the garden. When the Duke of Dunstable snorted, he held back nothing but gave it all he had.

'It wasn't a breach of promise!'

'What was it, then?'

'If you want to know, she said she knew where she could lay her hands on a couple of willing helpers who would pinch Emsworth's pig for me, so I engaged her services, and she demanded five hundred pounds for the job, cash down in advance, and I gave her a cheque for that sum.'

'Well, really!'

'What do you mean, Well, really? She wouldn't settle for less.'

'Then so far it would seem that she is the one who has put something over, as you express it.'

'That's what she thought, but she was mistaken. Immediately after coming to that arrangement I spoke of with Emsworth I got in touch with my bank and stopped the cheque. I telephoned the blighters and told them I'd scoop out their insides with my bare hands if they coughed up so much as a penny of it. I'd like to see her face when it comes back marked "Refer to drawer".'

It seemed to Lord Tilbury that from somewhere near at hand, as it might have been from behind those bushes near which he was sitting, there had come a sudden gasping sound as if uttered by some soul in agony, but he paid little attention to it. He was following a train of thought.

'So you have not had to pay anything for the pig?'

'Not a bean.'

'Then you ought to let me have it cheaper.'

'You think so, do you? Well, let me tell you, Stinker,' said the Duke, who had been deeply offended by his companion's remark about old fools, 'that my price for that pig has gone up. It's three thousand now.'

'What!'

'That's what it is. Three thousand pounds.'

A sudden hush seemed to have fallen on the garden of the Emsworth Arms. It was as though it and everything in it had been stunned into silence. Birds stopped chirping. Butterflies froze in mid-flutter. Wasps wading in strawberry jam paused motionless, as if they were having their photographs taken. And the general paralysis extended to Lord Tilbury. It was an appreciable time before he spoke. When he did, it was in the hoarse voice of a man unable to believe that he has heard correctly.

'You're joking!'

'Like blazes I'm joking.'

'You expect me to pay three thousand pounds for a pig?'

'If you want the ruddy pig.'

'What about our gentlemen's agreement?'

'Gentlemen's agreements be blowed. If you care to meet my

terms, the porker's yours. If you don't, I'll sell it back to Emsworth. No doubt he'll be glad to have it, even if the price is stiff. I'll leave you to think it over, Stinker. No skin off my nose,' said the Duke, 'whichever way you decide.'

CHAPTER NINE

I

Aman who has built up a vast business, starting from nothing, must of necessity be a man capable of making swift decisions, and until this moment Lord Tilbury had never had any difficulty in doing so. His masterful handling of the hundred and one problems that arise daily in a concern like the Mammoth Publishing Company was a byword in Fleet Street.

But as he sat contemplating the dilemma on the horns of which the Duke's parting words had impaled him, he was finding it impossible to determine what course to pursue. The yearning to enrol the Empress under his banner was very powerful, but so also was his ingrained dislike for parting with large sums of money. There was, and always had been, something about signing his name to substantial cheques that gave him a sort of faint feeling.

He was still weighing this against that and balancing the pros and cons, when a shadow fell on the sunlit turf before him and he became aware that his reverie had been intruded on. Something female was standing beside the rustic table, and after blinking once or twice he recognized his former secretary,

Lavender Briggs. She was regarding him austerely through her harlequin glasses.

If Lavender Briggs' gaze was austere, it had every reason for being so. No girl enjoys hearing herself described as tall and ungainly with large feet and hair like seaweed, especially if the description is followed up by the revelation that the five hundred golden pounds on which she had been counting to start her off as a proprietress of a typewriting bureau have gone with the wind, never to return. If she had not had a business proposition to place before him, she would not have lowered herself by exchanging words with this man. She would much have preferred to hit him on the head with the tankard from which the Duke had been refreshing himself. But a business girl cannot choose her associates. She has to take them as they come.

'Good afternoon, Lord Tilbury,' she said coldly. 'If you could spay-ah me a moment of your time.'

To any other caller without an appointment the owner of the Mammoth Publishing Company would have been brusque, but Lord Tilbury could not forget that this was the girl who had come within an ace of taking five hundred pounds off the Duke of Dunstable, and feeling as he did about the Duke he found his surprise at seeing her mingled with an unwilling respect. It would be too much to say that he was glad to see her, for he had hoped to continue wrestling undisturbed with the problem which was exercising his mind, but if she wanted a moment of his time, she could certainly have it. He even went so far as to ask her to take a seat, which she did. And having done so she came, like a good business woman, straight to the point.

'I heard what the Duke of Dunstable was saying to you,' she

said. 'This mattah of Lord Emsworth's pig. His demand for three thousand pounds was preposterous. Quate absurd. Do not dream of yielding to his terms.'

Lord Tilbury found himself warming to this girl. He still felt that the words in which he had described her hair, feet and general appearance had been well chosen, but we cannot all be Miss Americas and he was prepared to condone her physical defects in consideration of this womanly sympathy. Beauty, after all, is but skin deep. The main thing a man should ask of the other sex is that their hearts be in the right place, as hers was. 'Preposterous' . . . 'Quate absurd' . . . The very expressions he would have chosen himself.

On the other hand, it seemed to him that she was overlooking something.

'But I want that pig.'

'You shall have it.'

Enlightenment dawned on Lord Tilbury.

'Why, of course! You mean you'll – er –'

'Purloin it for you? Quate. My arrangements are all made and can be put into effect immediately.'

Lord Tilbury could recognize efficiency when he saw it. Here, he perceived, was a girl who thought on her feet and did it now. A genial glow suffused him. Almost as sweet as the thought of obtaining possession of the Empress was the knowledge that, to employ the latter's phrase, he would be putting one over on the Duke.

'Provided,' Lavender Briggs went on, 'that we agree on terms. I should requiah five hundred pounds.'

'Later, you mean?'

'Now, I mean. I know you always carry your cheque-book with you.'

Lord Tilbury gulped. Then the momentary sensation of nausea passed. Nothing could make him enjoy writing a cheque for five hundred pounds, but there are times when a man has to set his teeth and face the facts of life.

'Very well,' he said, a little huskily.

'Thank you,' said Lavender Briggs, a few moments later, placing the slip of paper in her bag. 'And now I ought to be getting back to the castle. Lady Constance may be wanting me for something. I will go and telephone for the station cab.'

The telephone by means of which residents of the Emsworth Arms put themselves in touch with the station cab (Jno. Robinson, propr.) was in the bar. Proceeding thither, Lavender Briggs was about to go in, when she nearly collided with Lord Ickenham, coming out.

2

Lord Ickenham had come to the bar of the Emsworth Arms because the warmth of the day had made him want to renew his acquaintance with G. Ovens' home-brew, of which he had many pleasant memories. It would have been possible – indeed, it would have been more seemly – for him to have taken tea on the terrace with Lady Constance, but he was a kindly man and something told him that after their recent get-together his hostess would prefer to be spared anything in the nature of peaceful co-existence with him. Moments came in a woman's life, he knew, when her prime need is a complete absence of Ickenhams.

He was glad to see Lavender Briggs. He was a man who made friends easily, and in the course of this visit to the castle, something approaching a friendship had sprung up between himself and her. And though he disapproved of her recent activities, he could understand and sympathize with the motives which had actuated them. He was a broad-minded man, and it was his opinion that a girl who needs five hundred pounds to set herself up in business for herself is entitled to stretch a point or two and to forget, if only temporarily, the lessons which she learned at her mother's knee. Thinking these charitable thoughts and knowing the reception that awaited her at Blandings Castle, he was happy to have this opportunity of warning her against completing her journey there.

'Well, well,' he said. 'So you're back?'

'Yayess. I caught the twelve-thirty train.'

'I wonder how it compares with the two-fifteen.'

'I beg your pardon?'

'Just a random thought. It was simply that I have heard the two-fifteen rather highly spoken of lately. Did you have a nice time in London?'

'Quate enjoyable, thank you.'

'I hope I didn't stop you going into that bar for a quick one?'

'I was merely intending to telephone for the station cab to take me to the castle.'

'I see. Well, I wouldn't. Are you familiar with the poem "Excelsior"?'

'I read it as a child,' said Lavender Briggs with a little shiver of distaste. She did not admire Longfellow.

'Then you will recall what the old man said to the fellow with the banner with the strange device. "Try not the pass," he said. "Dark lowers the tempest overhead." That is what an old – or rather, elderly but wonderfully well-preserved – man is saying to you now. Avoid station cabs. Lay off them. Leave them alone. You are better without them.'

'I don't know what you mean!'

'There are many things you do not know, Miss Briggs,' said Lord Ickenham gravely, 'including the fact that you have got a large smut on your nose.'

'Oh, have I?' said Lavender Briggs, opening her bag in a flutter and reaching hurriedly for her mirror. She plied the cleansing tissue. 'Is that better?'

'Practically perfect. I wish I could say as much for your general position.'

'I don't understand.'

'You will. You're in the soup, Miss Briggs. The gaff has been blown, and the jig is up. The pitiless light of day has been thrown on your pig-purloining plans. Bill Bailey has told all.'

'What!'

'Yes, he has squealed to the F.B.I. Where you made your mistake was in underestimating his integrity. These curates have scruples. The Reverend Cuthbert Bailey's are the talk of Bottleton East. Your proposition revolted him, and only the fact that you didn't offer him any kept him from spurning your gold. He went straight to Lord Emsworth and came clean. That is why I suggest that you do not telephone for station cabs in that light-hearted way. Jno. Robinson would take you to your destination for a reasonably modest sum, no doubt, but what would you find there on arrival? A Lord Emsworth with all his passions roused and flame coming out of both nostrils. For don't deceive yourself into thinking that he will be waiting on the front doorstep with a "Welcome to Blandings Castle" on his lips. In his current role of sabre-toothed tiger he would probably bite several pieces out of your leg. I have seldom seen a man who had got it so thoroughly up his nose.'

Lavender Briggs' jaw had fallen. So, slipping from between

her nerveless fingers, had her bag. It fell to earth, and from it there spilled a powder compact, a handkerchief, a comb, a lipstick, a match box, an eyebrow pencil, a wallet with a few pound notes in it, a small purse containing some shillings, a bottle of digestive pills, a paperback copy of a book by Alfred Camus and the Tilbury cheque. A little breeze which had sprung up sent the last-named fluttering across the road with Lord Ickenham in agile pursuit. He recovered it, glanced at it, and brought it back to her, his eyebrows raised.

'Your tariff for stealing pigs comes high,' he said. 'Who's Tilbury? Anything to do with Tilbury House?'

There was good stuff in Lavender Briggs. Where a lesser woman would have broken down and wept, she merely hitched up her fallen jaw and tightened her lips.

'He owns it,' she said, taking the cheque. 'I used to be his secretary. Lord Tilbury.'

'Oh, that chap? Good heavens, what are you doing?'

'I'm tearing up his cheque.'

Lord Ickenham stopped her with a horrified gesture.

'My dear child, you mustn't dream of doing such a thing. You need it in your business.'

'But I can't take his money now.'

'Of course you can. Stick to it like glue. He has far too much money, anyway, and it's very bad for him. Look on adhering to this five hundred as a kindly act in his best interests, designed to make him a better, deeper man. It may prove a turning point in his life. I would take five hundred pounds off Tilbury myself, if only I could think of a way of doing it. I should feel it was my duty. But if you have scruples, though you haven't any business having any, not being a curate, look on it as a loan. You could even pay him interest. Not too much, of course. You don't want to spoil him. I would suggest a yearly fiver, accompanied, as a pretty gesture, by a bunch of white violets. But you can think that over at your leisure. The problem that presents itself now, it seems to me, is Where do you go from here? I take it that you will wish to return to London, but you don't want another stuffy journey in the train. I'll tell you what,' said Lord Ickenham, inspired. 'We'll hire a car. I'll pay for it, and you can reimburse me when that typewriting bureau of yours gets going. Don't forget the bunch of white violets.'

'Oh, Lord Ickenham!' said Lavender Briggs devoutly. 'What a help you are!'

'Help is a thing I am always glad to be of,' said Lord Ickenham in his courteous way.

3

As he turned from waving a genial hand at the departing car and set out on the two-mile walk back to the castle, Lord Ickenham was feeling the gentle glow of satisfaction which comes to a man of goodwill conscious of having acted for the best. There had been a moment when his guardian angel, who liked him to draw the line somewhere, had shown a disposition to become critical of his recent activities, whispering in his ear that he ought not to have abetted Lavender Briggs in what, in the guardian angel's opinion, was pretty raw work and virtually tantamount to robbery from the person, but he had his answer ready. Lavender Briggs, he replied in rebuttal, needed the stuff, and when you find a hard-up girl who needs the stuff, the essential thing is to see that she gets it and not to be fussy about the methods employed to that end.

This, moreover, he pointed out, was a special case. As he had reminded La Briggs, it was imperative for the good of his soul that Lord Tilbury should receive an occasional punch in the bank balance, and to have neglected this opportunity of encouraging his spiritual growth would have been mistaken kindness. His guardian angel, who could follow a piece of reasoning all right if you explained it carefully to him, apologized and said he hadn't thought of that. Forget the whole thing, the guardian angel said.

With the approach of evening the day had lost much of its oppressive warmth, but Lord Ickenham kept his walking pace down to a quiet amble, strolling in leisurely fashion and pausing from time to time to inspect the local flora and fauna: and he had stopped to exchange a friendly glance with a rabbit whose looks he liked, when he became aware that there were others more in tune than himself with the modern spirit of rush and bustle. Running footsteps sounded from behind him, and a voice was calling his name. Turning, he saw that the Duke of Dunstable's nephew, Archie Gilpin, was approaching him at a high rate of m.p.h.

With Archie's brother Ricky, the poet, who supplemented the meagre earnings of a minor bard by selling onion soup in a bar off Leicester Square, Lord Ickenham had long been acquainted, but Archie, except for seeing him at meals, he scarcely knew. Nevertheless, he greeted him with a cordial smile. The urgency of his manner suggested that here was another fellow human being in need of his advice and counsel, and, as always, he was delighted to give it. His services were never confined to close personal friends.

'Hullo there,' he said. 'Getting into training for the village sports?'

Archie came to a halt, panting. He was a singularly handsome young man. Pongo at the Milton Street registry office had described him as good-looking, but Lord Ickenham, now that he had met him, considered this an understatement. Tall and slim and elegant, he looked like a film star of the better type. He also, Lord Ickenham was sorry to see, looked worried, and he prepared to do all that was in his power to brighten life for him.

Archie seemed embarrassed. He ran a hand through his hair, which was longer than Lord Ickenham liked hair to be. A visit to a hairdresser would in his opinion have done this Gilpin a world of good. But artists, he reminded himself, are traditionally shy of the scissors, and to do the lad justice he did not wear sideburns.

'I say,' said Archie, when he had finished panting. 'Could you spare me a moment?'

'Dozens, my dear fellow. Help yourself.'

'I don't want to interrupt you, if you're thinking about something.'

'I am always thinking about something, but I can switch it off in a second, just like that. What seems to be the trouble?'

'Well, I'm in a bit of a jam, and my brother Ricky once told me that if ever I got into a jam of any kind, you were the man to get me out of it. When it comes to fixing things, he said, you have to be seen to be believed.'

Lord Ickenham was gratified as any man would have been. One always likes a word of praise from the fans.

'He probably had in mind the time when I was instrumental in getting him the money that enabled him to buy that onion soup bar of his. Oddly enough, it was not till I had it explained to me by my nephew Pongo that I knew what an onion soup bar was. My life is lived in the country, and we rustics so soon get out of touch. Pongo tells me these bars abound in the Piccadilly Circus and Leicester Square neighbourhoods of London, staying open all night and selling onion soup to the survivors of bottle parties. It sounds the ideal life. Is Ricky still gainfully employed in that line?'

'Oh, rather. But may I tell you about my jam?'

Lord Ickenham clicked an apologetic tongue.

'Of course, yes. I'm sorry. I'm afraid we old gaffers from the country have a tendency to ramble on. When I start talking you must stop me, even if you haven't heard it before. This jam of yours, you were saying. Not a bad jam, I trust?'

Once more, Archie Gilpin ran a hand through his hair. The impression he conveyed was that if the vultures gnawing at his bosom did not shortly change their act, he would begin pulling it out in handfuls.

'It's the dickens of a jam. I don't know what to do about it. Have you ever been engaged to two girls at the same time?'

'Not to my recollection. Nor, now I come to think of it, do I know of anyone who has, except of course King Solomon and the late Brigham Young.'

'Well, that's what I am.'

'You? Engaged to two girls? Half a second, let me work this out.'

There was a pause, during which Lord Ickenham seemed to be doing sums in his head.

'No,' he said at length. 'I don't get it. I am aware that you are betrothed to my little friend Myra Schoonmaker, but however often I tot up the score, that only makes one. You're sure you haven't slipped up somewhere in your figures?'

Archie Gilpin's eye rolled in a fine frenzy, glancing from

heaven to earth, from earth to heaven, though one would more readily have expected that sort of thing from his poetic brother.

'Look here,' he said. 'Could we sit down somewhere? This is going to take some time.'

'Why, certainly. There should be good sitting on that stile over there. And take all the time you want.'

Seated on the stile, his deportment rather like that of a young Hindu fakir lying for the first time on the traditional bed of spikes, Archie Gilpin seemed still to find a difficulty in clothing his thoughts in words. He cleared his throat a good deal and once more disturbed his hair with a fevered hand. He reminded Lord Ickenham of a nervous after-dinner speaker suddenly aware, after rising to his feet, that he has completely forgotten the story of the two Irishmen, Pat and Mike, on which he had been relying to convulse his audience.

'I don't know where to begin.'

'At the beginning, don't you think? I often feel that that is best. Then work through the middle and from there, taking your time, carry on to the end.'

This appeared to strike Archie Gilpin as reasonable. He became a little calmer.

'Well, it started with old Tilbury. You know I had a job on one of old Tilbury's papers?'

'Had?'

'He fired me last week.'

'Too bad. Why was that?'

'He didn't like a caricature I'd drawn of him.'

'You shouldn't have shown it to him.'

'I didn't, not exactly. I showed it to Millicent. I thought she would get a laugh out of it.'

'Millicent?'

'His secretary. Millicent Rigby. Girl I was engaged to.'

'That you *were* engaged to?'

'Yes. She broke it off.'

'Of course, yes,' said Lord Ickenham. 'I remember now that Pongo told me he had met a fellow who knew a chap who was acquainted with Miss Rigby, and she had told him – the chap, not the fellow – that she had handed you the pink slip. What had you done to incur her displeasure? You showed her this caricature, you say, but why should that have offended her? Tilbury, if I followed you correctly, was its subject, not she.'

A curious rumbling sound told Lord Ickenham that his companion had uttered a hollow groan. It occurred to him, as the other's hand once more shot to his head, that if this gesture was to be repeated much oftener, Archie, like Lady Constance, would have to go to Shrewsbury for a hair-do.

'Yes, I know. Yes, that's right. But I ought to have mentioned that, thinking Tilbury was out at lunch, I went and showed it to her in his office. I put it on his desk, and we were looking at it with our heads together.'

'Ah,' said Lord Ickenham, beginning to understand. 'And he wasn't out at lunch? He came back?'

'Yes.'

'Saw your handiwork?'

'Yes.'

'Took umbrage?'

'Yes.'

'And erased your name from the list of his skilled assistants?'

'Yes. It was his first move. And later on Millicent ticked me off in no uncertain manner for being such a fool as to bring the thing into the old blighter's office, because anyone but a perfect idiot would have known that he was bound to come in, and hadn't I any sense at all, and . . . Oh, well, you know what happens when a girl starts letting a fellow have it. One word led to another, if you know what I mean, and it wasn't long before she was breaking the engagement and telling me she didn't want to see or speak to me again in this world or the next. She didn't actually return the ring, because I hadn't given her one, but apart from that she made the thing seem pretty final.'

Lord Ickenham was silent for a moment. He was thinking of the six times his Jane had done the same thing by him years ago, and he knew how the other must be feeling.

'I see,' he said. 'Well, my heart bleeds for you, my poor young piece of human wreckage, but this bears out what I was saying, that the sum total of your fiancées is not two, but one. It's nice to have got that straight.'

Another hollow groan escaped Archie Gilpin. His hand rose, but Lord Ickenham caught it in time.

'I wouldn't,' he said. 'Don't touch it. It looks lovely.'

'But you don't know what happened just now. You could have knocked me down with a toothpick. I was coming along by the Emsworth Arms, and I saw her.'

'Miss Rigby?'

'Yes.'

'Probably a mirage.'

'No she was there in the flesh.'

'What in the world was she doing in Market Blandings?'

'Apparently old Tilbury came here for some reason . . .'

Lord Ickenham nodded. He knew that reason.

'. . . and he brought her with him, to do his letters. She had popped out for a breath of air, and I came along, and we met, face to face, just about opposite the Jubilee Memorial watering-trough in the High Street.'

'Dramatic.'

'I was never so surprised in my life.'

'I can readily imagine it. Was she cold and proud and aloof?'

'Not by a jugful. She was all over me. Remorse had set in. She said she was sorry she had blown a fuse, and wept a good deal and . . . well, there we were, so to speak.'

'You folded her in your embrace, no doubt?'

'Yes, quite a good deal, actually, and the upshot of the whole thing was that we got engaged again.'

'You didn't mention that you were engaged to Myra?'

'No, I didn't get around to that. The subject didn't seem to come up somehow.'

'I quite understand. So the total is two, after all. You were perfectly right, and I apologize. Well, well!'

'I don't see what you're grinning about.'

'Smiling gently would be a more exact description. I was thinking how absurdly simple these problems are, when you give your mind to them. The solution here is obvious. You must at once tell Myra to make no move in the way of buying the trousseau and pricing wedding cakes, because they won't be needed.'

Only a sudden clutch at the rail on which he was seated prevented Archie Gilpin from falling off the stile. It seemed for a moment that he was about to reach for his hair again, but he merely gaped like a goodlooking codfish.

'Tell her it's all off, you mean?'

'Precisely. Save the girl a lot of unnecessary expense.'

'But I can't. I admit that I asked her to marry me because I was feeling pretty bitter about Millicent and had some sort of rough idea of showing her –'

'That she was not the only onion in the stew?'

'Something on those lines. And I was considerably relieved when she turned me down. A narrow escape, I felt I'd had. But now that on second thoughts she's decided that she's in favour of the scheme, I don't see how I can possibly just stroll in and tell her I've changed my mind. Well, dash it, is a shot like that on the board? I ask you!'

'You mean that once a Gilpin plights his troth, it stays plighted? A very creditable attitude to take, though it's a pity you plight it so often. But if you are thinking you may break that gentle heart, have no uneasiness. I can state authoritatively that, left to herself, she wouldn't marry you with a ten-foot pole.'

'Then why did she tell me she would?'

'For precisely the reason that made you propose to her. Relations were strained between her and her betrothed, just as they were between you and Miss Rigby, and she did it as what is known as a gesture. She thought, in a word, that that would teach him.'

'She's got a betrothed?'

'And how! You know him. My friend Meriwether.'

'Good Lord!' Archie Gilpin seemed to blossom like a rose in June. 'Well, this is fine. You've eased my mind.'

'A pleasure.'

'Now one begins to see daylight. Now one knows where one is. But, look here, we don't want to do anything . . . what's the word?'

'Precipitate?'

'Yes, we want to move cautiously. You see, on the strength

of getting engaged to the daughter of a millionaire I'm hoping to extract a thousand quid from Uncle Alaric.'

Lord Ickenham pursed his lips.

'From His Grace the pop-eyed Duke of Dunstable? No easy task. His one-way pockets are a byword all over England.'

Archie nodded. He had never blinded himself to the fact that anyone trying to separate cash from the Duke of Dunstable was in much the same position as a man endeavouring to take a bone from a short-tempered wolf-hound.

'I know. But I have a feeling it will come off. When I told him I was engaged to Myra, he was practically civil. I think he's ripe for the touch, and I've simply got to get a thousand pounds.'

'Why that particular sum?'

'Because that's what Ricky wants, to let me into his onion soup business. He's planning to expand, and has to have more capital. He said that if I put in a thousand quid, I could have a third share of the profits, which are enormous.'

'Yes, so Pongo told me. I got the impression of dense crowds of bottle-party addicts charging into Ricky's bar night after night like bisons making for a water-hole.'

'That's right, they do. There's something about onion soup that seems to draw them like a magnet. Can't stand the muck myself but there's no accounting for tastes. Here's the set-up, as I see it,' said Archie, with mounting enthusiasm. 'We coast along as we are at present, Myra engaged to me, me engaged to Myra, and Uncle Alaric fawning on me and telling me I can have anything I want, even unto half his kingdom. I get the thousand quid. Myra gives me the push. I slide off and marry Millicent. Myra marries this Meriwether chap, and everybody's happy. Any questions?'

A look of regret and pity had come into Lord Ickenham's face. It pained him to be compelled to act as a black frost in this young man's garden of dreams, but he had no alternative.

'Myra can't give you the push.'

Archie stared. It seemed to him that this kindly old buster, until now so intelligent, had suddenly lost his grip.

'Why not?'

'Because the moment she did, she would be shipped back to America in disgrace and would never see Bill Bailey again.'

'Who on earth's Bill Bailey?'

'Oh, I forgot to tell you, didn't I? That – or, rather, the Reverend Cuthbert Bailey – is Meriwether's real name. He is here incognito because Lady Constance has a deep-seated prejudice against him. He is a penniless curate, and she doesn't like penniless curates. It was to remove Myra from his orbit that she took her away from London and imprisoned her at Blandings Castle. Let her break the engagement, and she'll be back in New York before you can say What ho.'

Silence fell. The light had faded from the evening sky, and simultaneously from Archie Gilpin's face. He sat staring bleakly into the middle distance as if the scenery hurt him in some tender spot.

'It's a mix-up,' he said.

'It wants thinking about,' Lord Ickenham agreed. 'Yes, it certainly wants thinking about. We must turn it over in our minds from time to time.'

CHAPTER TEN

I

The Duke of Dunstable was not a patient man. When he had business dealings with his fellows, he liked those fellows to jump to it and do it now, and as a general rule took pains to ensure that they did so. But in the matter of Lord Tilbury and the Empress he was inclined to be lenient. He quite understood that a man in the position of having to make up his mind whether or not to pay three thousand pounds for a pig, however obese, needs a little time to think it over. It was only on the third day after the other's return to London that he went to the telephone and having been placed in communication with him opened the conversation with his customary 'Hoy!'

'Are you there, Stinker?'

If the Duke had not been a little deaf in the right ear, he might have heard a sound like an inexperienced motorist changing gears in an old-fashioned car. It was the proprietor of the Mammoth Publishing Company grinding his teeth. Sometimes, when we hear a familiar voice, the heart leaps up like that of the poet Wordsworth when he beheld a rainbow in the sky. Lord Tilbury's was far from doing this. He resented having his morning's work interrupted by a man capable of ignoring gentlemen's agreements and slapping an extra thousand pounds on the price of pigs. When he spoke, his tone was icy.

'Is that you, Dunstable?'

'What?'

'I said, Is that you?'

'Of course it's me. Who do you think it was?'

'What do you want?'

'What?'

'I said What do you want? I'm very busy.'

'What?'

'I said I am very busy.'

'So am I. Got a hundred things to do. Can't stand talking to you all day. About that pig.'

'What about it?'

'Are you prepared to meet my terms? If so, say so. Think on your feet, Stinker?'

Lord Tilbury drew a deep breath. How fortunate, he was feeling, that Fate should have brought him and Lavender Briggs together and so enabled him to defy this man as he ought to be defied. He had heard nothing from Lavender Briggs, but he presumed that she was at Blandings Castle, working in his interests, framing her subtle schemes, and strong in this knowledge he proceeded to answer in the negative. This took some time for in addition to saying 'No' he had to tell the Duke what he thought of him, indicating one by one the various points on which his character diverged from that of the ideal man. Whether it was right of him to call the Duke a fat old sharper whose word he would never again believe, even if given on a stack of Bibles, is open to debate, but he felt considerably better when he had done so, and it was with the feeling of having fought the good fight that several minutes later he slammed down the receiver and rang for Millicent Rigby to come and take dictation.

Nothing that anyone could say to him, no matter how derogatory, ever had the power to wound the Duke. After that initial 'No', indeed, he had scarcely bothered to listen. He could see that it was just routine stuff. All he was thinking, as he came away from the telephone, was that he would now sell the Empress back to Lord Emsworth, who he knew would prove co-operative, and he was proceeding in search of him when a loud squeak in his rear told him that little George was with him again.

'Hullo, big boy,' said George.

'How often have I told you not to call me big boy?'

'Sorry, chum, I keep forgetting. I say, frightfully exciting about Myra, isn't it?'

'Eh?'

'Getting engaged to Archie Gilpin.'

In the interest of his conversation with Lord Tilbury, the Duke had momentarily forgotten that his nephew had become betrothed to the only daughter of a millionaire. Reminded of this, he beamed, as far as it was within his ability to beam, and replied that it was most satisfactory and that he was very pleased about it.

'Her father arrives tomorrow.'

'Indeed?'

'Gets to Market Blandings station, wind and weather permitting, at four-ten. Grandpapa's gone to London to meet him, all dressed up. He looked like a city slicker.'

'You must not call your grandfather a city slicker,' said the

Duke, too happy at the way his affairs were working out for a sterner rebuke. He paused, for a sudden thought had struck him, and George, about to inquire whose grandfather he *could* call a city slicker, found himself interrupted. 'What made him get all dressed up and go to London to meet this feller?' he asked, for he knew how much his host disliked the metropolis and how great was his distaste for putting on a decent suit of clothes and trying to look like a respectable human being.

'Aunt Connie told him he jolly well had to or else. He was as sick as mud.'

The Duke puffed at his moustache. His nosiness where other people's affairs were concerned was intense, and Connie's giving this Yank what amounted to a civic welcome intrigued him. It meant something, he told himself. It couldn't be that she was trying to sweeten the feller in the hope of floating a loan, for she had ample private means, bequeathed to her by her late husband, Joseph Keeble, who had made a packet out East, so it must be that she entertained towards him feelings that were deeper and warmer than those of ordinary friendship, as the expression was. He had never suspected this, but it occurred to him now that when a woman keeps a photograph of a man with a head like a Spanish onion on her writing table, it means that her emotions are involved, in all probability deeply. There was that occasion, too, when he had joined them at luncheon at the Ritz. Their heads, he remembered, had been very close together. By the time he had succeeded in shaking off George, declining his invitation to come down to the lake and chat with the Church Lads, he was convinced that he had hit on the right solution, and he waddled off to find Lord Ickenham and canvass his views on the subject. He was not fond of Lord Ickenham, but there was nobody else available as a confidant.

He found him in his hammock, pondering over the various problems which had presented themselves of late, and lost no time in placing the item on the agenda paper.

'I say, Ickenham, this fellow who's coming here tomorrow. This chap Stick-in-the-mud.'

'Schoonmaker. Jimmy Schoonmaker.'

'You know him?'

'One of my oldest friends. I shall like seeing him again.'

'So will somebody else.'

'Who would that be?'

'Connie, that's who. Let me tell you something, Ickenham. I was in Connie's room yesterday, having a look round, and there was a cable on the writing table. "Coming immediately", it said, and a lot more I've forgotten. It was signed Schoonmaker, and was obviously a reply to a cable from her, urging him to come here. Now why was she in such a sweat to get the feller to Blandings Castle, you ask.'

'So I do. Glad you reminded me.'

'I'll tell you why. It sticks out a mile. She's potty about the chap. Sift the evidence. In spite of his having a head like a Spanish onion, she keeps his photograph on her writing table. She sends him urgent cables telling him to come immediately. And what is even more significant, she makes Emsworth put on a clean collar and go all the way to London to meet him. Why, dash it, she didn't do that for *me*! Would she go to such lengths if she wasn't potty about the . . . Get out, you!'

He was addressing Beach, who had approached the hammock and uttered a discreet cough.

'What you want?'

'I was instructed by her ladyship to inquire of his lordship if he would be good enough to speak to her ladyship in her ladyship's boudoir, your Grace,' said Beach with dignity. He was not a man to be put upon by Dukes, no matter how white-moustached.

'Wants to see him, does she?'

'Precisely, your Grace.'

'Better go and find out what it's all about, Ickenham. Remember what I was saying. Watch her closely!' said the Duke in a hissing whisper. 'Watch her like a hawk.'

There was a thoughtful look in Lord Ickenham's eye as he crossed the lawn. This new development interested him. He was aware how sorely persecuted Lord Emsworth was by his sister Constance – the other's story of the brass paper-fastener had impressed him greatly – and he had hoped by his presence at the castle to ease the strain for him a little, but he had never envisaged the possibility of actually removing her from the premises. If Lady Constance were to marry James Schoonmaker and go to live with him in America, it would be the biggest thing that had happened to Lord Emsworth since his younger son Frederick had transferred himself to Long Island City, N.Y., as a unit of the firm of Donaldson's Dog Biscuits, Inc. There is no surer way of promoting human happiness than to relieve a mild man of the society of a sister who says, 'Oh, Clarence!' to him and sees life in the home generally as a sort of Uncle Tom's Cabin production, with herself playing Simon Legree and her brother in the supporting role of Uncle Tom.

Of course, it takes two to make a romance, and James Schoonmaker had yet to be heard from, but Lord Ickenham regarded his old friend's instant response to Lady Constance's cable as distinctly promising. A man in Jimmy's position, a monarch of finance up to his eyes all the time in big deals, with barely a moment to spare from cornering peanuts or whatever it might be, does not drop everything and come bounding across the Atlantic with a whoop and a holler unless there is some great attraction awaiting him at the other end. It would be a good move, he decided, when Jimmy arrived, to meet him at Market Blandings station, hurry him off to the Emsworth Arms and fill him to the brim with G. Ovens' home-brewed beer. Mellowed by that wonder fluid, he felt, it was more than likely that he would cast off reserve, become expansive and give a sympathetic buddy what George Cyril Wellbeloved would have called the griff.

Lady Constance was seated at her writing table, tapping the woodwork with her fingers, and Lord Ickenham had the momentary illusion, as always when summoned to her presence, that time had rolled back in its flight and that he was once more *vis-à-vis* with his old kindergarten mistress. The great question in those days had always been whether or not she would rap him on the knuckles with a ruler, and it was with some relief that he noted that the only weapon within his hostess's reach was a small ivory paper-knife.

She was not looking cordial. Her air was that of somebody who, where Ickenhams were concerned, could take them or leave them alone. A handsome woman, though, and one well calculated to touch off the spark in the Schoonmaker bosom.

'Please sit down, Lord Ickenham.'

He took a chair, and Lady Constance remained silent for a moment. She seemed to be searching for words. Then, for she was never a woman who hesitated long when she had something to say, even when that something verged on the embarrassing, she began.

'Myra's father is arriving tomorrow, Lord Ickenham.'

'So I had heard. I was saying to Dunstable just now how much I shall enjoy seeing him again after all these years.'

A slight frown on Lady Constance's forehead seemed to suggest that his emotions did not interest her.

'I wonder if Jimmy's put on weight. He was inclined to bulge when I last saw him. Wouldn't watch his calories.'

Nor, said the frown, was she in a mood to discuss Mr Schoonmaker's poundage.

'He has come because I asked him to. I sent him an urgent cable.'

'After we had had our little talk?'

'Yes,' said Lady Constance, shuddering as she recalled that little talk. 'I intended to put the whole matter in his hands and advise him to take Myra back to America immediately.'

'I see. Did you say so?'

'No, I did not, and I am particularly anxious that he shall know nothing of her infatuation. It would be difficult to explain why I had allowed Mr Bailey to stay on at the castle.'

'Very difficult. One can see him raising his eyebrows.'

'On the other hand, I must give him some reason why I sent that cable, and I wanted to see you, Lord Ickenham, to ask if you had anything to suggest.'

She sank back in her chair, stiffened in every limb. Her companion was beaming at her, and his kindly smile affected her like a blow in the midriff. She was in a highly nervous condition, and the last thing she desired was to be beamed at by a man whose very presence revolted her finer feelings.

'My dear Lady Constance,' said Lord Ickenham buoyantly,

'the matter is simple. I have the solution hot off the griddle. You tell him that his daughter has become engaged to Archie Gilpin and you wanted him to look in and give the boy the once-over. Perfectly natural thing to suggest to an affectionate father. He would probably have been very hurt, if you hadn't cabled him. That solves your little difficulty, I think?'

Lady Constance relaxed. Her opinion of this man had in no way altered, she still considered him a menace to one and all and his presence an offence to the pure air of Blandings Castle, but she was fair enough to admit that, however black his character might be, and however much she disliked having him beam at her, he knew all the answers.

2

The 11.45 train from Paddington, first stop Swindon, rolled into Market Blandings station, and Lord Emsworth stepped out, followed by James R. Schoonmaker of Park Avenue, New York, and The Dunes, Westhampton, Long Island.

American financiers come in all sizes, ranging from the small and shrimp-like to the large and impressive. Mr Schoonmaker belonged to the latter class. He was a man in the late fifties with a massive head and a handsome face interrupted about half way up by tortoiseshell-rimmed spectacles. He had been an All-American footballer in his youth, and he still looked capable of bucking a line, though today he would have done it not with a bull-like rush but with an authoritative glance which would have taken all the heart out of the opposition.

His face, as he emerged, was wearing the unmistakable look of a man who has had a long railway journey in Lord

Emsworth's company, but it brightened suddenly when he saw the slender figure standing on the platform. He stared incredulously.

'Freddie! Well, I'll be darned!'

'Hullo there, Jimmy.'

'You here?'

'That's right.'

'Well, well!' said Mr Schoonmaker.

'Well, well, well!' said Lord Ickenham.

'Well, well, well, *well*!' said Mr Schoonmaker.

Lord Emsworth interrupted the reunion before it could reach the height of its fever. He was anxious to lose no time in getting to the haven of his bedroom and shedding the raiment which had been irking him all day. His shoes, in particular, were troubling him.

'Oh, hullo, Ickenham. Is the car outside?'

'Straining at the leash.'

'Then let us be off, shall we?'

'Well, I'll tell you,' said Lord Ickenham. 'I can readily understand your desire to hasten homeward and get into something loose –'

'It's my shoes, principally.'

'They look beautiful.'

'They're pinching me.'

'The very words my nephew Pongo said that day at the dog races, and his statement was tested and proved correct. Courage, Emsworth! Think of the women in China. You don't find them beefing because their shoes are tight. But what I was about to say was that Jimmy and I haven't seen each other for upwards of fifteen years, and we've a lot of heavy thread-picking-up to do. I thought I'd take him to the

Emsworth Arms for a quick one. You'd enjoy a mouthful of beer, Jimmy?'

'Ah!' said Mr Schoonmaker, his tongue flickering over his lips.

'So we'll just bung you into the car and walk over later.'

The process of bunging Lord Emsworth into a car was never a simple one, for on these occasions his long legs always took on something of the fluid quality of an octopus's tentacles, but the task was accomplished at last, and Lord Ickenham led his old friend to a table in the shady garden where all those business conferences between Lord Tilbury, the Duke of Dunstable and Lavender Briggs had taken place.

'Ah!' said Mr Schoonmaker again some little time later, laying down his empty tankard.

'Have another?'

'I think I will,' said Mr Schoonmaker, speaking in the rather awed voice customary with those tasting G. Ovens' home-brewed for the first time. He added that the beverage had a kick, and Lord Ickenham agreed that its kick was considerable. He said he thought G. Ovens put some form of high explosive in it, and Mr Schoonmaker agreed that this might well be so.

A considerable number of threads had been picked up by this time, and it seemed to Lord Ickenham that it would not be long now before he would be able to divert the conversation from the past to the present. From certain signs he saw that the home-brewed was beginning to have its beneficent effect. Another pint, he felt, should be sufficient to bring his companion to the confidential stage. In one of the cosy talks he had had with George Cyril Wellbeloved before Lord Emsworth had driven him with a flaming sword from his garden of Eden, the pigman had commented on the mysterious properties of a quart of the Ovens output, speaking with a good deal of bitterness of the time when that amount of it had caused him to reveal to Claude Murphy, the local constable, certain top secrets which later he would have given much to have kept to himself.

The second pint arrived, and Mr Schoonmaker quaffed deeply. His journey had been a stuffy one, parching to the throat. He looked about him approvingly, taking in the smooth turf, the shady trees and the silver river that gleamed through them.

'Nice place, this,' he said.

'Rendered all the nicer by your presence, Jimmy,' replied Lord Ickenham courteously. 'What brought you over here, by the way?'

'I had an urgent cable from Lady Constance.' A thought struck Mr Schoonmaker. 'Nothing wrong with Mike, is there?'

'Not to my knowledge. Nor with Pat. Mike who?'

'Myra.'

'I didn't know she was known to the police as Mike. You must have started calling her that after my time. No, Myra's all right. She's just got engaged.'

Mr Schoonmaker started violently, always a dangerous thing to do when drinking beer. Having stopped coughing and dried himself off, he said:

'She has? What made her do that?'

'Love, Jimmy,' said Lord Ickenham with a touch of reproach. 'You can't expect a girl not to fall in love in these romantic surroundings. There's something in the air of Blandings Castle that brings out all the sentiment in people. Strong men have come here without a thought of matrimony in their minds and within a week have started writing poetry and carving hearts on trees. Probably the ozone.'

Mr Schoonmaker was frowning. He was not at all sure he liked the look of this. His daughter's impulsiveness was no secret from him.

'Who is the fellow?' he demanded, not exactly expecting to hear that it was the boy who cleaned the knives and boots, but prepared for the worst. 'Who's this guy she's got engaged to?'

'Gilpin is the name, first name Archibald. He's the nephew of the Duke of Dunstable,' said Lord Ickenham, and Mr Schoonmaker's brow cleared magically. He would have preferred not to have a son-in-law called Archibald, but he knew that in these matters one has to take the rough with the smooth, and he had a great respect for Dukes.

'Is he, by golly! Well, that's fine.'

'I thought you'd be pleased.'

'When did this happen?'

'Oh, recently.'

'Odd that Lady Constance didn't mention it in her cable.'

'Probably wanted to keep the expense down. You know what they charge you per word for cables, and a penny saved is a penny earned. Do you call her Lady Constance?'

'Of course. Why not?'

'Rather formal. You've known her a long time.'

'Yes, we've been friends for quite a while, very close friends as a matter of fact. She's a wonderful woman. But there's a sort of cool aristocratic dignity about her . . . a kind of aloofness . . . I don't know how to put it, but she gives you the feeling that you'll never get to first base with her.'

'And you want to get to first base with her?' said Lord Ickenham, eyeing him narrowly. Mr Schoonmaker had just finished his second pint, and something told him that this was the moment for which he had been waiting. It was after his second pint that George Cyril Wellbeloved had poured out his confidences to Constable Claude Murphy, among them his personal technique for poaching pheasants.

For an instant it seemed that Mr Schoonmaker would be reticent, but the Ovens home-brewed was too strong for him. A pinkness spread itself over his face. The ears, in particular, were glowing brightly.

'Yes, I do,' he said, glaring a little as if about to ask Lord Ickenham if he wanted to make something of it. 'Why shouldn't I?'

'My dear fellow, I'm not criticizing. I'm all sympathy and understanding. Any red-blooded man would be glad to get to first base with Connie.'

Mr Schoonmaker started.

'Do you call her Connie?'

'Of course.'

'How do you manage it?'

'Just comes naturally.'

'I wish it did to me.' Mr Schoonmaker looked into his tankard, saw that it was empty and heaved a long sigh. 'Yes, sir, I wish I had your nerve. Freddie, if I could get that woman to marry me, I'd be the happiest man on earth.'

With the exception, Lord Ickenham thought, as he laid a gentle hand on his friend's arm, of her brother Clarence.

'Now you're talking, Jimmy. Relay that information to her. Women like to hear these things.'

'But I told you. I haven't the nerve.'

'Nonsense. A child of six could do it, provided he hadn't got the dumb staggers.'

Mr Schoonmaker sighed again. G. Ovens' home-brewed tends as a rule to induce joviality – sometimes, as in the case of George Cyril Wellbeloved, injudicious joviality – but it was plain that today it had failed of its mission.

'That's just what I have got. When I try to propose to her, the words won't come. It's happened a dozen times. The sight of that calm aristocratic profile wipes them from my lips.'

'Try not looking at her sideways.'

'I'm not in her class. That's the trouble. I'm aiming too high.'

'A Schoonmaker is a fitting mate for the highest in the land.'

'Who says so?'

'I say so.'

'Well, I don't. I know what would happen. She'd be very nice about it, but she would freeze me.'

Lord Ickenham, who had removed his hand from the arm, replaced it.

'Now there I'm sure you're wrong, Jimmy. I happen to be certain that she loves you. Connie has few secrets from me.'

Mr Schoonmaker stared.

'You aren't telling me she told you she did?'

'Not in so many words, of course. You could hardly expect that, even to an old friend like myself. But that way she has of drawing her breath in sharply and looking starry-eyed whenever your name is mentioned is enough to show me how things stand. The impression I received was of a woman wailing for her demon lover. Well, perhaps not actually wailing, but making quite a production number of it. I tell you I've seen her clench her hands till the knuckles stood out white under the strain, just because your name happened to come up in the course of conversation. I'm convinced that if you were to try the Ickenham system, you couldn't fail.'

'The Ickenham system?'

'I call it that. It's a little thing I knocked together in my bachelor days. It consists of grabbing the girl, waggling her about a bit, showering kisses on her upturned face and making some such remark as "My mate!". Clench the teeth of course, while saying that. It adds conviction.'

Mr Schoonmaker's stare widened.

'You expect me to do that to *Lady Constance*?'

'I see no objection.'

'I do.'

'Such as −?'

'I couldn't even get started.'

'Where's your manly courage?'

'I don't have any, not where she's concerned.'

'Come, come. She's only a woman.'

'No, she isn't. She's Lady Constance Keeble, sister of the Earl of Emsworth, with a pedigree stretching back to the Flood, and I can't forget it.'

Lord Ickenham mused. He recognized the fact that an obstacle had arisen, but a few moments' thought told him that it was not an impasse.

'What you need, Jimmy, is a pint or two of May Queen.'

'Eh?'

'It is a beverage which I always recommend to timorous wooers when they find a difficulty in bringing themselves to try the Ickenham system. Its full name is "Tomorrow'll be of all the year the maddest, merriest day, for I'm to be Queen of the May, mother, I'm to be Queen of the May", but the title is generally shortened for purposes of convenience in ordinary conversation. Its foundation is any good dry champagne, to which is added liqueur brandy, kummel and green chartreuse, and I can assure you it acts like magic. Under its influence little men with receding chins and pince-nez have dominated the proudest beauties and compelled them to sign on the dotted line. I'll tell Beach to see that you get plenty of it before and during dinner tonight. Then you take Connie out on the terrace under the moon and go into the Ickenham routine, and I shall be vastly surprised if we don't shortly see an interesting announcement in *The Times*.'

'H'm.' Mr Schoonmaker weighed the suggestion, but it was plain that he was none too enthusiastic about it. 'Grab her?'

'That's it.'

'Waggle her about?'

'That's the idea.'

'And say "My mate!"?'

'Unless there is some other turn of phrase which you prefer,' said Lord Ickenham, always ready to stretch a point. 'You needn't stick too closely to the script if you feel like gagging, but on no account tamper with the business. That is of the essence.'

3

On the morning following his old friend's arrival, Lord Ickenham had settled himself in his hammock when a husky voice spoke his name and he found Mr Schoonmaker at his side. Sitting up and directing a keen glance at him, he did not like what he saw. James Schoonmaker was looking pale and careworn, and there was in his bearing no suggestion whatsoever that he was the happiest man on earth. He looked, indeed, far more like that schooner Hesperus of which Lord Ickenham in his boyhood had recited so successfully, on the occasion when it swept like a sheeted ghost to the reef of Norman's Woe. Give him a skipper and a little daughter whom he had taken to bear him company, thought Lord Ickenham, and he could have made straight for the reef of Norman's Woe, and no questions asked.

But he was too well-bred to put this sentiment into words. Instead, he affected an eager animation which he was far from feeling.

'Jimmy! I was hoping you would come along. Have you good news to report? Everything pretty smooth? I start saving up for the wedding present?'

Mr Schoonmaker shook his head and simultaneously uttered a sharp cry of anguish. As Lord Ickenham had suspected, he was in no shape to shake heads. To the dullest eye it would have been plain that this hand across the sea was in the grip of a hangover of majestic proportions.

'That May Queen is kind of powerful stuff,' said Mr Schoonmaker, endorsing this view.

'It sometimes brings regrets with the dawning of a new day,' Lord Ickenham agreed. 'It's the chartreuse mostly, I think. Still, if it has produced results . . .'

'But it hasn't.'

'Come, come, Jimmy. With my own eyes I saw you lead Connie out on to the terrace, and the moon was shining like billy-o.'

'Yes, and what happened? What always happens, and what's always going to happen. I lost my nerve.'

Lord Ickenham sighed. This was a set-back, and though he

knew that these disappointments are sent to us to make us more spiritual, he could never bring himself to like them.

'You didn't ask her to marry you?'

'I didn't come within a mile of it.'

'What *did* you talk about? The weather?'

'We talked about Mike and this boy she's engaged to. I asked her why she hadn't mentioned him in her cable.'

'What did she say to that?'

'She said she wanted to wait till I could see him for myself. Seems strange.'

'Nothing strange about it. She could hardly tell you that she sent the cable because she couldn't endure being away from you for another minute. Modesty forbade.'

For a moment Mr Schoonmaker brightened.

'You really think that was it?'

'Of course it was. She loves you with every fibre of her being. She's crazy about you. So cheer up, Jimmy, and have another pop when you're feeling better. My experience is that a May Queen hangover soon wears off after one has had a little sleep. Try this hammock.'

'Don't you want it?'

'Your need is greater than mine.'

'Well, thanks,' said Mr Schoonmaker. The momentary brightness seemed to ooze out of him as he climbed into the hammock, leaving him the pessimist he had been. He heaved a sigh. 'Of course, you're all wrong, Freddie. There's no hope for me. I know when I'm licked.'

'Scarcely the spirit of '76.'

'She would never consider me for a moment. We don't play in the same league. Oh well,' said Mr Schoonmaker, heaving another sigh, 'there's always one's work.'

A sudden gleam came into Lord Ickenham's eye. It was as if a thought had occurred to him.

'What are you working on now, Jimmy? Something big, of course?'

'Fairly big. Do you know Florida?'

'Not very well. My time in America was spent out west and in New York.'

'Then you probably don't know Jupiter Island.'

'I've heard of it. Sort of a winter home from home for millionaires, isn't it?'

'That kind of idea. Club, golf links, tennis, bathing. You rent a cottage for the season.'

'And pay pretty high for it, no doubt?'

'Yes, it comes high. This thing I'm promoting is the same sort of set-up farther down the coast. The Venus Island Development Corporation, it's called. There'll be a fortune in it.'

'You aren't looking for capital, I suppose?'

'No difficulty there. Why?'

'I was only thinking, Jimmy, that as your daughter is marrying his nephew, it would be a graceful act to let the Duke in on the ground floor. He's rolling in money, but he can always do with a bit more. There's something about the stuff that fascinates him.'

Mr Schoonmaker was on the verge of sleep, but he was sufficiently awake to reply that he would be glad to do the Duke this good turn. He thanked Lord Ickenham for the suggestion and Lord Ickenham said he always made a point of doing his day's kind deed. His mother, he said, had been frightened by a Boy Scout.

'I expect to pass through this world but once, Jimmy. Any

good thing, therefore, that I can do, let me do it now, as the fellow said. How's the hammock?'

Mr Schoonmaker snored gently, and Lord Ickenham went off to have a word with the Duke.

CHAPTER ELEVEN

I

The Duke of Dunstable was sitting on the terrace, and not only on the terrace but on top of the world with a rainbow round his shoulder. Counting his blessings one by one, he was of the opinion that he had never had it so good. He had not yet approached Lord Emsworth in the matter of the Empress, but he knew that when he did he would be in the pleasant position of dealing in a seller's market. And he had the comforting thought that, whatever the figure arrived at, it would be all clear profit, with none of the distasteful necessity of paying agent's commission. The recollection of how nearly he had come to parting with that five hundred pounds to Lavender Briggs still made him shudder.

And in addition to this, showing that when Providence starts showering its boons on a good man, the sky is the limit, his nephew Archibald, until now a sad burden on his purse, was engaged to be married to the only daughter of a millionaire. How the young poop had done it, he was at a loss to understand, but there it was, and so deep was his contentment that when Lord Ickenham dropped into a chair beside him, he did not even puff at his moustache. He disliked Lord

Ickenham, considering him a potty sort of feller whose spiritual home was a padded cell in some not too choosy lunatic asylum, but this morning he was the friend of all the world.

Lord Ickenham was looking grave.

'Hope I'm not interrupting you, Dunstable, if you were doing the crossword puzzle.'

'Not at all,' said the Duke amiably. 'I was only thinkin' a bit.'

'I'm afraid I've come to give you more food for thought,' said Lord Ickenham, 'and not very agreeable thought, either. It's very saddening, don't you feel, how people change for the worse as the years go on?'

'Who does? I don't.'

'No, not you. You always maintain a safe suds level. I was thinking of poor Schoonmaker.'

'What's poor about him?'

There was a look of pain on Lord Ickenham's face. He was silent for a moment, musing, or so it seemed, on life's tragedies.

'Everything,' he said. 'When I knew James Schoonmaker fifteen years ago in New York, he was a man with a glittering future, and for a time, I understand, he did do extremely well. But that's all in the past. He's gone right under.'

'Under what?' said the Duke, who was never very quick at the uptake.

'He's a pauper. Down to his last thirty cents. Please don't mention this to anyone, but he's just been borrowing money from me. It was a great shock.'

The Duke sat up. This time he did not neglect to puff at his moustache. It floated up like a waterfall going the wrong way.

'But he's a millionaire!'

Lord Ickenham smiled sadly.

'That's what he'd like you to believe. But I have friends in New York who keep me posted from time to time about the fellows I used to know there, and they have told me his whole story. He's down to his last dollar, and his bankruptcy may be expected at any moment. You know how it is with these American financiers. They over-extend themselves. They bite off more than they can chew, and then comes the inevitable smash. A fiver means a lot to Schoonmaker at this moment. A tenner was what he wanted just now, and I gave it to him, poor devil. I hadn't the heart to refuse. This is strictly between you and me, of course, and I wouldn't like it to be spread about, but I thought I ought to warn you about him.'

The Duke's eyes were protruding like a snail's. His moustache was in a constant state of activity. Not even little George had ever seen it giving so sedulously of its best.

'Warn me? If the feller thinks he's going to get tuppence out of *me*, he'll be disappointed.'

'He's hoping for more than tuppence. I'm afraid he's planning to try to talk you into putting up money for some wild-cat scheme he's got. As far as I could make out, it's some sort of land and building operation down in Florida. The Venus Island Development Corporation he calls it. The very name sounds fishy, don't you think? Venus Island, I mean to say! There probably isn't such a place. What's worrying me is that you may feel tempted to invest, because he'll make the thing sound so good. He's very plausible. But don't dream of doing it. Be on your guard.'

'I'll be on my guard,' said the Duke, breathing heavily.

Lord Ickenham waited a moment in case the other might wish to thank his benefactor, but as he merely continued to breathe heavily, he made his way back to the hammock. He found Mr Schoonmaker sitting up and looking brighter. He was glad to hear that his nap had done him good.

'Headache gone?'

Mr Schoonmaker considered this.

'Well, not gone,' he said. He was a man who liked exactness of speech. 'But it's a lot better.'

'Then what I wish you would do, Jimmy, is go and see the Duke and tell him all about that Venus Island thing of yours. I've just been talking to him, and oddly enough, he was saying he wished he could find some business opportunity which would give him the chance of having a little flutter. He's a great gambler at heart.'

Mr Schoonmaker disapproved of his choice of words. A man with a hangover of the dimensions of the one from which he was suffering finds it difficult to bridle, but he did his best.

'Gambler? What do you mean, gambler? The Venus Island Development Corporation's as sound as Fort Knox.'

'I'm sure it is,' said Lord Ickenham soothingly. 'Impress that on him. Give him a big sales talk.'

'Why?' said Mr Schoonmaker, still ruffled. 'I don't want his money.'

'Of course you don't. You'll be doing him a great favour by allowing him to buy in. But for goodness' sake don't let him see that. You know how proud these Dukes are. They hate to feel under an obligation to anyone. Seem eager, Jimmy.'

'Oh, all right,' said Mr Schoonmaker grudgingly. 'Though it's funny having to wheedle someone into accepting shares in something that'll quadruple his money in under a year.'

'We'll have a good laugh about it later,' Lord Ickenham assured him. 'You'll find him on the terrace,' he said. 'I told him you might be looking in.'

He nestled into the vacated hammock, and was in the process of explaining to his guardian angel, who had once more become critical, that there is no harm in deviating from the truth a little, if it is done in a good cause, and that the interview which Mr Schoonmaker was about to have with the Duke of Dunstable, though possibly wounding to his feelings, would make him forget his headache, when he became aware of Archie Gilpin at his side.

Archie was looking as beautiful as ever, but anxious.

'I say,' he said. 'I saw you talking to Uncle Alaric.'

'Yes, we had a chat.'

'What sort of mood is he in?'

'He seemed to me a little agitated. He was annoyed because an attempt was being made to get money out of him.'

'Oh, my God!'

'Or, rather, he was expecting such an attempt to be made. That always does something to the fine old man. Did you ever read a book called *The Confessions of Alphonse*, the reminiscences of a French waiter? No, I suppose not, for it was published a number of year ago, long before you were born. At one point in it Alphonse says "Instantly as a man wishes to borrow money of me, I dislike him. It is in the blood. It is more strong than me." The Duke's like that.'

Archie Gilpin reached for his hair and was busy for awhile with the customary scalp massage. There was a bleakness in his voice when at length he spoke.

'Then you wouldn't recommend an immediate try for that thousand?'

'Not whole-heartedly. But what's your hurry?'

'I'll tell you what's my hurry. I had a letter from Ricky this morning. He says he can only give me another week to raise the money. If I don't give it him by then, he'll have to get somebody else, he says.'

'A nuisance, I agree. That kind of ultimatum is always unpleasant. But much may happen in a week. Much, for that matter, may happen in a day. My advice to you –'

But Archie was not destined to receive that advice, which would probably have been very valuable, for at this moment Mr Schoonmaker appeared, and he sidled off. The father of his betrothed, now that he had made his acquaintance, always gave him a sort of nervous feeling akin to what are sometimes called the heeby-jeebies and he was never completely at his ease in his presence. It was the tortoiseshell-rimmed spectacles principally that did it, he thought, though possibly the square jaw contributed its mite.

Mr Schoonmaker stood looming over the hammock like a thundercloud.

'You and your damned Dukes!' he said and Lord Ickenham raised his eyebrows.

'My dear Jimmy! It may be my imagination, but a certain half-veiled something in your manner seems to suggest that your conference with Dunstable was not an agreeable one. What happened? Did you broach the subject of the Venus Island Development Corporation?'

'Yes, I did,' said Mr Schoonmaker, taking time out for a snort similar in its resonance to the shot heard round the world. 'And he acted as if he thought I was some sort of con man. Did you tell him I'd borrowed money from you?'

Lord Ickenham's eyes widened. He was plainly at a loss.

'Borrowed money from me? Of course not.'

'He said you did.'

'How very extraordinary. How much am I supposed to have lent you?'

'Ten pounds.'

'What a laughable idea! The sort of sum a man like you leaves on the plate for the waiter when he's had lunch. What on earth can have put that into his head?' Lord Ickenham's face cleared. 'I'll tell you what I think must have misled him, Jimmy. I remember now that I was talking to him about the old days in New York, when we were both young and hard up and I would sometimes sting you for a trifle and you would sometimes sting me for a trifle, according to which of us happened to have anything in his wallet at the moment, and he got it all mixed up. Very muddle-headed man, the Duke. His father, I believe, was the same. So were his sisters and his cousins and his aunts. Well, I must say the thought of someone of your eminence panhandling me for a tenner is a very stimulating one. It isn't everyone who gets his ear bitten by a millionaire. How did you leave things with Dunstable?'

'I told him he was crazy and came away.'

'Very proper. And what are you planning to do now?'

A faint blush spread itself over Mr Schoonmaker's face.

'I thought I might go and see if Lady Constance would like a stroll in the park or something.'

'Connie,' Lord Ickenham corrected. 'You won't get anywhere if you don't think of her as Connie.'

'I won't get anywhere if I do,' said Mr Schoonmaker morosely.

The morning was now pleasantly warm and full of little soothing noises, some contributed by the local insects, others by a gardener who was mowing a distant lawn, and it was not long after Mr Schoonmaker's departure before Lord

Ickenham's eyes closed and his breathing became soft and regular. He was within two breaths of sleep, when a voice spoke.

'Hoy!' it said, and he sat up.

'Hullo, Dunstable. You seem upset.'

The Duke's eyes were popping, and his moustache danced in the breeze.'

'Ickenham, you were right!'

'About what?'

'About that Yank, that feller Stick-in-the-Mud. Not ten minutes after you'd warned me he was going to do it, he came to me and started trying to get me to put up money for that Tiddlypush Island scheme of his.'

Lord Ickenham gave a low whistle.

'You don't say!'

'That's what he did.'

'So soon! One would have expected him to wait at least till he had got to know you a little better. He was very plausible, of course?'

'Yes, very.'

'He would be. These fellows always specialize in the slick sales talk. You weren't taken in, I hope?'

'*Me?*'

'No, of course not. You're much too level-headed.'

'I sent him off with a flea in his ear, by Jove!'

'I see. I don't blame you. Still, it's very embarrassing.'

'Who's embarrassed? I'm not.'

'I was only thinking that as your nephew is going to marry his daughter . . .'

The Duke's jaw fell.

'Good God! I'd forgotten that.'

'I should try to bear it in mind from now on, if I were you, for it is a matter that affects you rather deeply. It's lucky you're a rich man.'

'Eh?'

'Well, you're going to have to support Archie and the girl, and not only them but Schoonmaker and his sisters. I believe he has three of them.'

'I won't do it!'

'Can't let them starve.'

'Why not?'

'You mean you think we all eat too much nowadays? Quite true, but it won't do you any good if they go about begging crusts of bread and telling people why. Can't you see the gossip columns in Tilbury's papers? They'd really spread themselves.'

The Duke clutched at the hammock, causing Lord Ickenham to oscillate and feel a little seasick. He had overlooked this angle, and none knew better than he how blithely, after what had occurred between them, the proprietor of the Mammoth Publishing Company would spring to the task of getting a certain something of his own back.

A thought struck him.

'Why should Archibald beg crusts of bread?'

'Wouldn't you, if suffering from the pangs of hunger?'

'He has a salaried position.'

'No longer.'

'Eh?'

'They handed him his hat.'

'His hat? How do you mean, his hat?'

'Putting it another way, his services were dispensed with last week.'

'What!'

'So he told me.'

'He never said anything about it to me.'

'Probably didn't want to cause you anxiety. He's a very considerate young man.'

'He's a poop and a waster!'

'I like his hair, though, don't you? Well, that's how matters stand, and I'm afraid it's going to cost you a lot of money. I don't see how you're going to do it under two or three thousand a year. For years and years and years. Great drain on your resources. What a pity it isn't possible for you just to tell Archie to break the engagement. That would solve everything. But of course you can't do it.'

'Why can't I? It's an excellent idea. I'll go and find him now, and if he raises the slightest objection, I'll kick his spine up through his hat.'

'No, wait. You still haven't got that toehold on the situation which I should like to see. You're forgetting the breach of promise case.'

'What breach of promise case?'

Lord Ickenham's manner was that of a patient governess explaining a problem in elementary arithmetic to a child who through no fault of its own had been dropped on the head when a baby.

'Isn't it obvious? If Archie were to break the engagement, the girl's first move would be to start an action for breach of promise. Even if the idea didn't occur to her independently, a man like Schoonmaker would see that she did it, and the jury would give her heavy damages without leaving the box. Archie tells me he has written her any number of letters.'

'How can he have written her letters when they're staying in the same dashed house?'

'Notes would perhaps be a better term. Fervid notes slipped into her hand by daylight or pushed under her door at night. You know what lovers are.'

'Sounds potty.'

'But is frequently done, I believe, when the heart is young.'

'He may not have mentioned marriage.'

'I wouldn't build too much on that. I know he asked me once how to spell "honeymoon", which shows the trend his thoughts were taking. You can't speak of honeymoons in a letter to a girl without laying up trouble for yourself. When you consider what a mere reference to chops and tomato sauce did to Mr Pickwick –'

'Who's Mr Pickwick?'

'Let it pass. I'm only saying that when those notes are read out in court, you'll be for it.'

'Why, me? If Archibald is fool enough to get involved in a breach of promise case, blast his idiotic eyes. I don't have to pay his damages.'

'It won't look well in the gossip columns, if you don't. He's your nephew.

The Duke uttered a bitter curse on all nephews, and Lord Ickenham agreed that they could be trying, though his own nephew Pongo, he said, held the view that all the trouble in the world was caused by uncles.

'I can see only one ray of hope.'

'What's that?' asked the Duke, who was unable to detect even one. His prominent eyes gleamed a little. He was saying to himself that this feller Ickenham might be potty, but apparently he had lucid intervals.

'It may be possible to buy the girl off. We have this in our favour, that she isn't in love with Archie.'

'Who could be in love with a poop like that?'

'Hers is rather a sad case. You know Meriwether?'

'The feller with the face?'

'A very accurate description. He has a heart of gold, too, but you don't see that.'

'What about him?'

'He is the man she wants to marry.'

'Meriwether is?'

'Yes.'

'Then why did she get engaged to Archibald?'

'My dear Dunstable! A girl whose father is on the verge of bankruptcy has to look out for herself. She isn't in a position to let her heart rule her head. When she has the opportunity of becoming linked by marriage to a man like you, you can't expect her not to grab it.'

'That's true.'

'She would much prefer not to make a marriage of convenience, but she sees no hope of happiness with the man she loves. What stands in the way of her union to Meriwether is money.'

'Hasn't he got any? You told me he came from Brazil. Fellers make money in Brazil.'

'He didn't. A wasting sickness struck the Brazil nuts, and he lost all his capital.'

'Silly ass.'

'Your sympathy does you credit. Yes, his lack of money is the trouble. And the reason I think Myra Schoonmaker would jump at any adequate offer is that he has just got the chance of buying into a lucrative onion soup business.'

The Duke started as if stung. The last three words always stirred him to his depths.

'My nephew Alaric runs an onion soup business.'

'No, really?'

'That's what he does. Writes poetry and sells onion soup. It embarrasses me at the club. Fellers come up to me and ask, "What's that nephew of yours doing now?", thinking I'm going to say he's in the diplomatic service or something, and I have to tell them he's selling onion soup. Don't know which way to look.'

'I can understand your emotion. The stuff is very nourishing, I believe, but, as far as I know, no statue has ever been erected to a man who sold onion soup. Still, there's lots of money in it, and this chap I'm speaking of is doing so well that he wants to expand. He has offered Meriwether a third share in his business for a thousand pounds. So if you were to offer the girl that . . .'

'A thousand pounds?'

'That's what Meriwether told me.'

'It's a great deal of money.'

'That's why the chap wants it.'

The Duke pondered. His was a slow mind, and it was only gradually that he ever grasped a thing. But he had begun to see what this Ickenham feller was driving at.

'You think that if I give the girl a thousand pounds, she'll pass it on to this gargoyle chap, and then she'll hand Archibald his hat and marry the gargoyle?'

'Exactly. You put it in a nutshell.'

A sudden healing thought came to the Duke. It was that if he bought the dashed girl off for a thousand and got three thousand from Emsworth for that appalling pig, he would still be comfortably ahead of the game. If it had been within his power to give people grateful looks, he would have given Lord

Ickenham one, for it appeared to him that he had found the way.

'I'll go and write the cheque now,' he said.

It seemed to Lord Ickenham, drowsing in his hammock after the Duke's departure, that an angel voice was speaking his name, and he speculated for a moment on the possibility of his having been snatched up to heaven in a fiery chariot without noticing it. Then reason told him that an angel, punctilious as all angels are, would scarcely on so brief an acquaintance be addressing him as Uncle Fred, and he sat up, brushing the mists of sleep from his eyes, to see Myra Schoonmaker standing beside him. She was looking as attractive as always, but her clothes struck him as unsuitable for a morning in the country.

'Hullo, young Myra,' he said. 'Why all dressed up?'

'I'm going to London. I came to ask if there was any little present I could bring you back.'

'Nothing that I can think of except tobacco. What's taking you to London?'

'Father has given me a big cheque and wants me to go and buy things.'

'A kindly thought. You don't seem very elated.'

'Not much to be elated about these days. Everything's such a mess.'

'Things will clear up.'

'Says you!'

'I would call the outlook rather promising.'

'Well, I don't know where you get that idea, but I wish you would sell it to Bill. He needs a bracer.'

'Morale low?'

'Very low. He's all jumpy. You know how you feel when you're waiting for something to explode.'

'Apprehensive?'

'That's the word. He can't understand why Lady Constance has said nothing to him.'

'Was he expecting a chat with her?'

'Well, wouldn't you in his place? He told Lord Emsworth who he was, and Lord Emsworth must have told her.'

'Not necessarily. Perhaps he forgot.'

'Could he forget a thing like that?'

'There is no limit to what Emsworth can forget, especially when he's distracted about his pig.'

'What's wrong with the pig? She looked all right to me when I saw her last.'

'What's wrong is that the Duke has taken her from him.'

'How?'

'It's a long story. I'll tell you about it some other time. What train are you catching?'

'The ten-thirty-five. I wanted Bill to sneak down to the station and come with me. I thought we might get married.'

'Very sensible. Wouldn't he?'

'No. He had scruples. He said it would be a low trick to play on Archie.'

Lord Ickenham sighed.

'Those scruples! They do keep popping up, don't they? Tell him to relax. Archie's dearest wish is to marry a girl named Millicent Rigby. He's engaged to her.'

'But he's engaged to me.'

'He's engaged to both of you. Very awkward situation for the poor boy.'

'Then why doesn't he just break it off?'

'He wants to get a thousand pounds out of the Duke to buy into an onion soupery, and he felt that if he jilted the daughter of a millionaire, his chances would be slim. His only course seemed to him to be to sit tight and hope for the best. And you can't break the engagement because Jimmy would take you back to America. Until this morning the situation was an extraordinarily delicate one.'

'What happened this morning?'

'The Duke somehow or other got the curious idea that your father was on the verge of bankruptcy, and he saw himself faced with the prospect of having to support not only you and Archie but the whole Schoonmaker family. His distaste for this was so great that he left me just now to go and write a cheque for a thousand pounds, payable to you. He hopes to buy you off.'

'Buy me off?'

'So that you won't sue Archie for breach of promise. When you see him, accept the cheque in full settlement, endorse it to Archie, and pay it into his bank. You'll just have time, if the train isn't late. Be sure to do it today. The Duke has a nasty habit of stopping cheques. Then, if you explain the situation to him, it is possible that Bill might see his way to joining you on that 10.35 train, and you and he could look in at the registry office tomorrow, being very careful this time to choose the same one. It would wind everything up very neatly.'

There was a silence. Myra drew a deep breath.

'Uncle Fred, did you work this?'

Lord Ickenham seemed surprised.

'Work it?'

'Did you tell the Duke Father was broke?'

Lord Ickenham considered.

'Well, now you mention it,' he said, 'it is just possible that some careless word of mine may have given him that impression. Yes, now that I think back, I believe I did say something along those lines. It seemed to me to come under the head of spreading sweetness and light. I thought I would be making everybody happy, except perhaps the Duke.'

'Oh, Uncle Fred!'

'Quite all right, my dear.'

'I'm going to kiss you.'

'Nothing to stop you, as far as I can see. Tell me,' said Lord Ickenham, when this had been done, 'do you think you can now overcome those scruples of Bill's?'

'I'll overcome them.'

'Just as well, perhaps, that he'll be leaving Blandings Castle. Never outstay your welcome, I always say. Then all that remains is to write a civil note to Lady Constance, thanking her for her hospitality, placing the facts before her and hoping that this finds her in the pink, as it leaves you at present. Give it to Beach. He'll see that she gets it. Why the light laugh?'

'It was more a giggle. I was thinking I'd like to see her face, when she reads it.'

'Morbid, but understandable. I'm afraid she may not be too pleased. There is always apt to be that trouble when you start spreading sweetness and light. You find there isn't enough to go around and someone has to be left out of the distribution. Very difficult to get a full hand.'

3

In supposing that, having given audience to the Duke, Mr Schoonmaker, Archie Gilpin and Myra, he would now be allowed that restful solitude which was so necessary to him when digesting the morning eggs and bacon, Lord Ickenham was in error. This time it was not an angel voice that interrupted his slumber, but more of a bleat, as if an elderly sheep in the vicinity had been endowed with speech. Only one man of his acquaintance bleated in just that manner, and he was not surprised, on assuming an upright pose, to find that it was Lord Emsworth who had been called to his attention. The ninth earl was drooping limply at his side, as if some unfriendly hand had removed his spinal column.

Having become reconciled by now to being in the position of a French monarch of the old régime holding a levee, Lord Ickenham showed no annoyance, but greeted him with a welcoming smile and said that it was a nice day.

'The sun,' he said, indicating it.

Lord Emsworth looked at the sun, and gave it a nod of approval.

'I came to give you something.'

'The right spirit. It's not my birthday, but I am always open to receive presents. What sort of something?'

'I'm sorry to say I've forgotten.'

'Too bad.'

'I shall remember it in time, I expect.'

'I'll count the minutes.'

'And there's something I wanted to tell you.'

'But you've forgotten it?'

'No, I remember that. It is about the Empress. I have been

thinking it over, Ickenham, and I have decided to buy the Empress from Dunstable. I admit I hesitated for awhile, because his price was so stiff. He is asking three thousand pounds.'

It took a great deal to disturb Lord Ickenham's normal calm, but at these words he could not repress a gasp.

'Three thousand *pounds*! For a pig?'

'For the Empress,' Lord Emsworth corrected in a reverent voice.

'Kick him in the stomach!'

'No, I must have the Empress, no matter what the cost. I am lost without her. I'm on the way to see her now.'

'Who's attending to her wants now that Wellbeloved's gone?'

'Oh, I've taken Wellbeloved back,' said Lord Emsworth, looking a little sheepish, as a man will who has done the weak thing. 'I had no alternative. The Empress needs constant care and attention, and no pigman I have ever had has understood her as Wellbeloved does. But I gave him a good talking to. And do you know what he said to me? He said something that shocked me profoundly.'

Lord Ickenham nodded.

'These rugged sons of the soil don't always watch their language. They tend at times to get a bit Shakespearian. What did he call you?'

'He didn't call me anything.'

'Then what shocked you?'

'What he said. He said that Briggs woman who bribed him to steal the Empress was in the pay of Dunstable. It was Dunstable she was working for. I was never so astounded in my life. Should I tax him about it, do you think?'

'In the hope of making him shave his price a bit?' Lord Ickenham shook his head. 'I doubt if that would get you anywhere. He would do what I always advise everyone to do, stick to stout denial. All you have to go on is Wellbeloved's word, and that would not carry much conviction. I like George Cyril Wellbeloved and always enjoy exchanging ideas with him, but I wouldn't believe his word if he brought it to me on a plate with watercress round it. On this occasion he probably deviated from the policy of a lifetime and told the truth, but what of that? You know and I know that Dunstable is a man who sticks at nothing and would walk ten miles in the snow to chisel a starving orphan out of tuppence, but we are helpless without proof. If only he had written some sort of divisional orders, embodying his low schemes in a letter, it would be –'

'Oh!' said Lord Emsworth.

'Eh?' said Lord Ickenham.

'I've just remembered what it was I came to give you,' said Lord Emsworth, feeling in his pocket. 'This letter. It got mixed up with mine. Well, I'll be getting along and seeing the Empress. Would you care to come?'

'Come? Oh, I see what you mean. I think not, thanks. Later on, perhaps.'

Lord Ickenham spoke absently. He had opened the letter, and a glance at the signature had told him that its contents might well be fraught with interest.

His correspondent was Lavender Briggs.

CHAPTER TWELVE

I

The door of Lady Constance's boudoir flew open and something large and spectacled shot out, so rapidly that it was only by an adroit *pas seul* that Beach, who happened to be passing at the moment, avoided a damaging collision.

'Oops!' said Mr Schoonmaker, for the large spectacled object was he. 'Pardon me.'

'Pardon me, sir,' said Beach.

'No, no, pardon me,' said Mr Schoonmaker.

'Very good, sir,' said Beach.

He was regarding this man who had so nearly become his dancing partner with a surprise which he did not allow to appear on his moonlike features, for butlers are not permitted by the rules of their guild to look surprised. Earlier in the day he had viewed Mr Schoonmaker with some concern, thinking that his face seemed pale and drawn, as if he were suffering from a headache, but now there had been a magical change and it was plain that he had made a quick recovery. The cheeks glowed, and the eyes, formerly like oysters in the last stages of dissolution, were bright and sparkling. Exuberant was the word Beach would have applied to the financier, if he had happened to know it. He had once heard Lord Ickenham use the expression 'All spooked up with zip and vinegar', and it was thus that he was mentally labelling Mr Schoonmaker now. Unquestionably spooked up, was his verdict.

'Oh, Beach,' said Mr Schoonmaker.

'Sir?' said Beach.

'Lovely day.'

'Extremely clement, sir.'

'I'm looking for Lord Ickenham. You seen him anywhere?'

'It was only a few moments ago that I observed his lordship entering the office of Lord Emsworth's late secretary, sir.'

'Late?'

'Not defunct, sir. Miss Briggs was dismissed from her post.'

'Oh, I see. Got the push, did she? Where is this office?'

'At the far end of the corridor on the floor above this one. Should I escort you there, sir?'

'No, don't bother. I'll find it. Oh, Beach.'

'Sir?'

'Here,' said Mr Schoonmaker, and thrusting a piece of paper into the butler's hand he curvetted off like, thought Beach, an unusually extrovert lamb in springtime.

Beach looked at the paper, and being alone, with nobody to report him to his guild, permitted himself a sharp gasp. It was a ten-pound note, and it was the third piece of largesse that had been bestowed on him in the last half hour. First, that charming young lady, Miss Schoonmaker, giving him a missive to take to her ladyship, had accompanied it with a fiver, and shortly after that Mr Meriwether had pressed money into his hand with what looked to him like a farewell gesture, though he had not been notified that the gentleman was leaving. It all seemed very mysterious to Beach, though far from displeasing.

Mr Schoonmaker, meanwhile, touching the ground only at odd spots, had arrived at Lavender Briggs' office. He found Lord Ickenham seated at the desk, and burst immediately into speech.

'Oh, Freddie. The butler told me you were here.'

'And he was quite right. Here I am, precisely as predicted. Take a chair.'

'I can't take a chair, I'm much too excited. You don't mind me walking about the room like this? I wanted to see you, Freddie. I wanted you to be the first to hear the news. Do you remember me telling you that if I could get Lady Constance to be my wife, I'd be the happiest man on earth?'

'I remember. Those were your very words.'

'Well, I am.'

Something of the bewilderment recently exhibited by Beach showed itself on Lord Ickenham's face. This was a totally unexpected development. A shrewd judge of form, he had supposed that only infinite patience and a compelling series of pep talks would have been able to screw this man's courage to the sticking point and turn him, as he appeared to have been turned, into a whirlwind wooer. Very unpromising wedding bells material his old friend had seemed to him in the previous talks they had had together, and he had almost despaired of bringing about the happy ending. For if a suitor's nerve fails him every time he sees the adored object sideways, it is seldom that he can accomplish anything constructive. Yet now it was plain that something had occurred to change James Schoonmaker from the timorous rabbit he had been to a dasher with whom Don Juan would not have been ashamed to shake hands. It struck him instantly that there could be but one solution of the mystery.

'Jimmy, you've been at the May Queen again.'

'I have not!'

'You're sure?'

'Of course I'm sure.'

'Well, I'm glad to hear that, for it is not a practice I would recommend so early in the day. And yet you tell me that you have been proposing marriage with, I am glad to hear, great success. How did you overcome that diffidence of yours?'

'I didn't have to overcome it. When I saw her sitting there in floods of tears, all my diffidence vanished. I felt strong and protective. I hurried to where she sat.'

'And grabbed her?'

'Certainly not.'

'Waggled her about?'

'Nothing of the kind. I bent over her and took her hand gently in mine. "Connie," I said.'

'Connie?'

'Certainly.'

'At last! I knew you would get around to it sooner or later. And then?'

'She said, "Oh, James!"'

'Well, I don't think much of the dialogue so far, but perhaps it got brighter later on. What did you say after that?'

'I said, "Connie, darling. What's the matter?"'

'One can understand how you must have been curious to know. And what was the matter?'

Mr Schoonmaker, who had been pacing the floor in the manner popularized by tigers at a zoo, suddenly halted in mid-stride, and the animation died out of his face as though turned off with a switch. He looked like a man suddenly reminded of something unpleasant, as indeed he had been.

'Who's this guy Meriwether?' he demanded.

'Meriwether?' said Lord Ickenham, who had had an idea that the name would be coming up shortly. 'Didn't Connie tell you about him?'

'Only that you brought him here.'

Lord Ickenham could understand this reticence. He recalled that his hostess, going into the matter at their recent conference, had decided that silence was best. It would have been difficult, as she had said, were she to place the facts before her betrothed, to explain why she had allowed Bill to continue enjoying her hospitality.

'Yes, I brought him here. He's a young friend of mine. His name actually is Bailey, but he generally travels incognito. He's a curate. He brushes and polishes the souls of the parishioners of Bottleton East, a district of London, where he is greatly respected. I'll tell you something about Bill Bailey, Jimmy. I have an idea he's a good deal attracted by your daughter Myra. Not easy to tell for certain because he wears the mask, but I wouldn't be at all surprised if he wasn't in love with her. One or two little signs I've noticed. Poor lad, it must have been a sad shock for him when he learned that she's going to marry Archie Gilpin.'

Mr Schoonmaker snorted. This habit of his of behaving like a bursting paper bag was new to Lord Ickenham. Probably, he thought, a mannerism acquired since his rise to riches. No doubt there was some form of unwritten law that compelled millionaires to act that way.

'She isn't,' said Mr Schoonmaker.

'Isn't what?'

'Going to marry Archie Gilpin. She eloped with Meriwether this morning.'

'You astound me. Are you sure? Where did you hear that?'

'She left a note for Connie.'

'Well, this is wonderful news,' said Lord Ickenham, his face lighting up. 'I'm not surprised you're dancing about all over the place on the tips of your toes. He's a splendid young fellow. Boxed three years for Oxford and, so I learn from a usually reliable source, went through the opposition like a dose of salts. I congratulate you, Jimmy.'

Mr Schoonmaker seemed to be experiencing some difficulty in sharing his joyous enthusiasm.

'I call it a disaster. Connie thinks so, too – that's why she was in floods of tears. And she says you're responsible.'

'Who, me?' said Lord Ickenham, amazed, not knowing that the copyright in those words was held by George Cyril Wellbeloved. 'What had I got to do with it?'

'You brought him here.'

'Merely because I thought he looked a little peaked and needed a breath of country air. Honestly, Jimmy,' said Lord Ickenham, speaking rather severely, 'I don't see what you're beefing about. If I hadn't brought him here, he wouldn't have eloped with Myra, thus causing Connie to burst into floods of tears, thus causing you to lose your diffidence and take her hand gently in yours and say "Connie, darling." If it hadn't been for these outside stimuli, you would still be calling her Lady Constance and wincing like a salted snail every time you saw her profile. You ought to be thanking me on bended knee, unless the passage of time has made you stiff in the joints. What's your objection to Bill Bailey?'

'Connie says he hasn't a cent to his name.'

'Well, you've enough for all. Haven't you ever heard of sharing the wealth?'

'I don't like Myra marrying a curate.'

'The very husband you should have wished her. The one thing a financier wants is a clergyman in the family. What happens next time the Senate Commission has you on the carpet and starts a probe? You say "As proof of my respectability, gentlemen, I may mention that my daughter is married to a curate. You don't find curates marrying into a man's family if there's anything fishy about him," and they look silly and apologize. And there's another thing.'

'Eh?' said Mr Schoonmaker, who had been musing.

'I said there was another thing you ought to bear in mind. Have you considered what would have happened if Myra had married the Duke of Dunstable's nephew? You would never have got Dunstable out of your hair. A Christmas present would have been expected yearly. You would have had to lunch with him, dine with him, be constantly in his society. He would have come over to New York to spend long visits with you. The children, if any, would have had to learn to call him "Uncle Alaric". I think you've been extraordinarily lucky, Jimmy. Imagine a life with Dunstable like a sort of Siamese twin.'

It is possible that Mr Schoonmaker would have had much to say in reply to this, for Lord Ickenham's reasoning, though shrewd, had not wholly convinced him that everything was for the best in the best of all possible worlds, but at this moment the air was rent by a stentorian 'Hoy!' and they perceived that the Duke of Dunstable was in their midst.

'Oh, *you're* here?' said the Duke, pausing in the doorway and giving Mr Schoonmaker a nasty look.

Mr Schoonmaker, returning the nasty look with accrued interest, said he was.

'I hoped you'd be alone, Ickenham.'

'Jimmy was just going, weren't you, Jimmy? This is your busy day, isn't it? A thousand things to attend to. So what,' said Lord Ickenham, as the door closed, 'can I do for you, Dunstable?'

The Duke jerked a thumb at the door.

'Has he been trying to touch you?'

'Oh, no. We were just talking.'

'Oh?'

The Duke transferred his gaze to the room, regarding it with dislike and disapproval. It had unpleasant memories for him. He took in the desk, the typewriter, the recording machine and the chairs with a smouldering eye. It was in this interior set, he could not but remember, that that woman with the spectacles had so nearly deprived him of five hundred pounds.

'What you doing here?' he asked, as if revolted to find Lord Ickenham in such surroundings.

'In Miss Briggs' office? I had a letter from her this morning asking me to look in and attend to a number of things on her behalf. She left, if you recall, in rather a hurry.'

'Why did she write to you?'

'I think she felt that I was her only friend at Blandings Castle.'

'You a friend of hers?'

'We became reasonably matey.'

'Then I'd advise you to choose your friends more carefully, that's what I'd advise you. Matey, indeed!'

'You don't like the divine Briggs?'

'Blasted female.'

'Ah, well,' said Lord Ickenham tolerantly, 'we all have our faults. Even I have been criticized at times. But you were going to tell me what you wanted to see me about.'

The Duke, who had been scowling at the typewriter, as if daring it to start something, became more composed. A curious gurgling noise suggested that he had chuckled.

'Oh, that? I just came to say that everything's all right.'

'Splendid. What's all right?'

'About the pipsqueak.'

'What pipsqueak would that be?'

'The Tiddlypush girl. She took the cheque.'

'She did?'

'In full settlement.'

'Well, that's wonderful news.'

'So there won't be any breach of promise case. She's gone to London.'

'Yes, I saw her for a moment before she left. You bought her off, did you?'

'That's what I did. "Here you are," I said, and I dangled the cheque in front of her. She didn't hesitate. Grabbed at it like a seal going after a slice of fish. I knew she would. They can't resist the cash. I've just been telling Archibald that she has . . . what's the expression you used when you told me he'd been sacked from that job of his?'

'Handed him his hat?'

'That's right. I told him she's handed him his hat.'

'Was he very distressed?'

'Didn't seem to be.'

'Easy come, easy go, he probably said to himself.'

'I shouldn't wonder. He's gone to London, too.'

'On the same train as Miss Schoonmaker?'

'No, he went in that little car of his. Said he was going to take a friend to dinner. Fellow of the name of Rigby.'

'Ah, yes, he has spoken to me of his friend Rigby. I believe they are very fond of each other.'

'Chap must be a silly ass if he's fond of a poop like Archibald.'

'Oh, we all have our likes and dislikes. You'll be leaving soon yourself, I take it?'

'Me? Why?'

'Well, it won't be very comfortable for you here now that Emsworth knows it was you who engaged Miss Briggs to steal his pig. Creates a strain, that sort of thing. Tension. Awkward silences.'

The Duke gaped. The shock had been severe. If a meteorite had entered through the open window and struck him behind one of his rather prominent ears, he might have been more taken aback, but not very much so. When he was able to speak, which was not immediately, he said:

'What . . . what you talking about?'

'Isn't it true?'

'Of course it's not true.'

Lord Ickenham clicked his tongue reprovingly.

'My dear Dunstable, I am always a great advocate of stout denial, but I'm afraid it is useless here. Emsworth has had the whole story from George Cyril Wellbeloved.'

The Duke was still feeling far from at his best, but he rallied sufficiently to say 'Pooh!'

'Who's going to believe him?'

'His testimony is supported by Miss Briggs.'

'Who's going to believe her?'

'Everybody, I should say. Certainly Emsworth, for one, after he hears this record.'

'Eh?'

'I told you I had received a letter from the divine Briggs this morning. In it she asked me to turn on her tape recording machine . . . this is the tape recording machine . . . because, she said, that would give the old bounder . . . I fancy she meant you . . . something to think about. I will now do so,' said Lord Ickenham. He pressed the button, and a voice filled the room.

'I, Alaric, Duke of Dunstable, hereby make a solemn promise, to you, Lavender Briggs . . .'

The Duke sat down abruptly. His jaw had fallen, and he seemed suddenly to have become as boneless as Lord Emsworth.

'. . . that if you steal Lord Emsworth's pig, Empress of Blandings, and deliver it to my home in Wiltshire, I will pay you five hundred pounds.'

'That,' said Lord Ickenham, 'is you in conference with La Briggs. She naturally took the precaution of having this instrument working at the time. It's always safer with these verbal agreements. Well, I don't know what view you take of the situation, but it seems to me that you and Emsworth are like two cowboys in the Malemute Saloon who have got the drop on each other simultaneously. You have young George's film, he has this Scotch tape or whatever it's called. I suggest a fair exchange. Or would you rather I brought Emsworth in here and played this recording to him? It's not a thing I would recommend. One feels that the consequences would be extremely unpleasant for you.'

The Duke froze, appalled. The feller was right. Let this get about, and not only would his name be a hissing and a byword, so that when he invited himself to houses in the future, his host and hostess would hasten to put their valuables away in a stout box and sit on the lid, but Emsworth would bring an action against him for conspiracy or malice aforethought or whatever it was and mulct him in substantial damages. With only the minimum of hesitation he thrust a hand in his pocket and produced the spool which had never left his person since little George had given it to him.

'Here you are, blast you!'

'Oh, thanks. Now everybody's happy. Emsworth has his pig, Myra her Bill, Archie his Millicent Rigby.'

The Duke started.

'His *what* Rigby?'

'Oh yes, I should have told you that, shouldn't I? He's gone to London to marry a very nice girl called Millicent Rigby, at least he says she's very nice, and he probably knows. By the way, that reminds me. There's one thing I wish you would clear up for me before you go. Why was it that you were so anxious that Archie shouldn't marry Myra Schoonmaker? It has puzzled me from the first. She's charming, and apart from being charming she's the heiress of one of the richest men in America. Don't you like heiresses?'

The Duke's moustache had become violently agitated. He was not normally quick-witted, but he had begun to suspect that fishy things had been going on. If this Ickenham had not been deliberately misleading him, he was very much mistaken.

'You told me Schoonmaker was broke!'

'Surely not?'

'You said he touched you for a tenner.'

'No, no, I touched *him* for a tenner. That may be where you got confused. What would a man like James Schoonmaker be doing, borrowing money from people? He's a millionaire, so Bradstreet informs us.'

'Who's Bradstreet?'

'The leading authority on millionaires. A sort of American Debrett. Bradstreet is very definite on the subject of James Schoonmaker. Stinking rich is, I believe, the expression it uses of him.'

The Duke continued to bend his brain to the problem. He was more convinced than ever that he had been deceived.

'Then why did she take that cheque?'

'Ah, that we shall never know. Just girlish high spirits, do you think?'

'I'll give her girlish high spirits!'

'I'll tell you a possible solution that has occurred to me. She knew that Archie was planning to get married and needed money, so being a kind-hearted girl she took the cheque and endorsed it over to him. Sort of a wedding present from you. Where are you going?'

The Duke had lumbered to the door. He paused with a hand on the handle, regarded Lord Ickenham balefully.

'I'll tell you where I'm going. I'm going to get to the telephone and stop that cheque.'

Lord Ickenham shook his head.

'I wouldn't. I still have the tape, remember. I was just about to give it to you, but if you are going to stop cheques, I shall have to make an agonizing reappraisal.'

There was silence, as far as silence was possible in a small room where the Duke was puffing at his moustache.

'You shall have it tomorrow night after the cheque has gone through. It's not that I don't trust you, Dunstable, it's simply that I don't trust you.'

The Duke breathed stertorously. He did not like many people, but he searched his mind in vain for somebody he disliked as much as he was disliking his present companion.

'Ickenham,' he said, 'you are a low cad!'

'Now you're just trying to be nice. I bet you say that to all the boys,' said Lord Ickenham, and rising from his chair he went off to tell Lord Emsworth that though he had lost Lavender Briggs and was losing a sister and the Duke of Dunstable, he would be gaining a pig which for three years in succession had won the silver medal in the Fat Pigs class at the Shropshire Agricultural Show.

There was a smile on his handsome face, the smile it always wore when he had given service.

P. G. Wodehouse

IN ARROW BOOKS

If you have enjoyed Blandings, you'll love Mr Mulliner

FROM

Mr Mulliner Speaking

The conversation in the bar-parlour of the Angler's Rest, which always tends to get deepish towards closing-time, had turned to the subject of the Modern Girl; and a Gin-and-Ginger-Ale sitting in the corner by the window remarked that it was strange how types die out.

'I can remember the days,' said the Gin-and-Ginger-Ale, 'when every other girl you met stood about six feet two in her dancing-shoes, and had as many curves as a Scenic Railway. Now they are all five foot nothing and you can't see them sideways. Why is this?'

The Draught Stout shook his head.

'Nobody can say. It's the same with dogs. One moment the world is full of pugs as far as the eye can reach; the next, not a pug in sight, only Pekes and Alsatians. Odd!'

The Small Bass and the Double-Whisky-and-Splash admitted that these things were very mysterious, and supposed we should never know the reason for them. Probably we were not meant to know.

'I cannot agree with you, gentlemen,' said Mr Mulliner. He had been sipping his hot Scotch and lemon with a rather abstracted air: but now he sat up alertly, prepared to deliver judgement. 'The reason for the disappearance of the dignified, queenly type of girl is surely obvious. It is Nature's method of ensuring the continuance of the species. A world full of the sort of young woman that Meredith used to put into his novels and du Maurier into his pictures in *Punch* would be a world full of permanent spinsters. The modern young man would never be able to summon up the nerve to propose to them.'

'Something in that,' assented the Draught Stout.

'I speak with authority on the point,' said Mr Mulliner, 'because my nephew, Archibald, made me his confidant when he fell in love with Aurelia Cammarleigh. He worshipped that girl with a fervour which threatened to unseat his reason, such as it was: but the mere idea of asking her to be his wife gave him, he informed me, such a feeling of sick faintness that only by means of a very stiff brandy and soda, or some similar restorative, was he able to pull himself together on the occasions when he contemplated it. Had it not been for ... But perhaps you would care to hear the story from the beginning?'

People who enjoyed a merely superficial acquaintance with my nephew Archibald (said Mr Mulliner) were accustomed to set him down as just an ordinary pin-headed young man. It was only when they came to know him better that they discovered their mistake. Then they realised that his pinheadedness, so far from being ordinary, was exceptional. Even at the Drones Club, where the average of intellect is not high, it was often said of Archibald that, had his brain been constructed of silk, he would have been hard put to it to find sufficient material to make a canary a pair of cami-knickers. He sauntered through life with a cheerful insouciance, and up to the age of twenty-five had only once been moved by anything in the nature of a really strong emotion – on the occasion when, in the heart of

Bond Street and at the height of the London season, he discovered that his man, Meadowes, had carelessly sent him out with odd spats on.

And then he met Aurelia Cammarleigh.

The first encounter between these two has always seemed to me to bear an extraordinary resemblance to the famous meeting between the poet Dante and Beatrice Fortinari. Dante, if you remember, exchanged no remarks with Beatrice on that occasion. Nor did Archibald with Aurelia. Dante just goggled at the girl. So did Archibald. Like Archibald, Dante loved at first sight: and the poet's age at the time was, we are told, nine – which was almost exactly the mental age of Archibald Mulliner when he first set eyeglass on Aurelia Cammarleigh.

Only in the actual locale of the encounter do the two cases cease to be parallel. Dante, the story relates, was walking on the Ponte Vecchia, while Archibald Mulliner was having a thoughtful cocktail in the window of the Drones Club, looking out on Dover Street.

And he had just relaxed his lower jaw in order to examine Dover Street more comfortably when there swam into his line of vision something that looked like a Greek goddess. She came out of a shop opposite the club and stood on the pavement waiting for a taxi. And, as he saw her standing there, love at first sight seemed to go all over Archibald Mulliner like nettlerash.

It was strange that this should have been so, for she was not at all the sort of girl with whom Archibald had fallen in love at first sight in the past. I chanced, while in here the other day, to pick up a copy of one of the old yellowback novels of fifty years ago – the property, I believe, of Miss Postlethwaite, our courteous and erudite barmaid. It was entitled *Sir Ralph's Secret*, and its heroine, the Lady Elaine, was described as a superbly handsome girl, divinely tall, with a noble figure, the arched Montresor nose, haughty eyes beneath delicately pencilled brows, and that indefinable air of aristocratic aloofness which marks the daughter of a hundred Earls. And Aurelia Cammarleigh might have been this formidable creature's double.

Yet Archibald, sighting her, reeled as if the cocktail he had just consumed had been his tenth instead of his first.

'Golly!' said Archibald.

To save himself from falling, he had clutched at a passing fellow-member: and now, examining his catch, he saw that it was young Algy Wymondham-Wymondham. Just the fellow-member he would have preferred to clutch at, for Algy was a man who went everywhere and knew everybody and could doubtless give him the information he desired.

'Algy, old prune,' said Archibald in a low, throaty voice, 'a moment of your valuable time, if you don't mind.'

He paused, for he had perceived the need for caution. Algy was a notorious babbler, and it would be the height of rashness to give him an inkling of the passion which blazed within his breast. With a strong effort, he donned the mask. When he spoke again, it was with a deceiving nonchalance.

'I was just wondering if you happened to know who that girl is, across the street there. I suppose you don't know what her name is in rough numbers? Seems to me I've met her somewhere or something, or seen her, or something. Or something, if you know what I mean.'

Algy followed his pointing finger and was in time to observe Aurelia as she disappeared into the cab.

'That girl?'

'Yes,' said Archibald, yawning. 'Who is she, if any?'

'Girl named Cammarleigh.'

'Ah?' said Archibald, yawning again. 'Then I haven't met her.'

'Introduce you if you like. She's sure to be at Ascot. Look out for us there.'

Archibald yawned for the third time.

'All right,' he said, 'I'll try to remember. Tell me about her. I mean, has she any fathers or mothers or any rot of that description?'

'Only an aunt. She lives with her in Park Street. She's potty.'

Archibald started, stung to the quick.

'Potty? That divine...I mean that rather attractive-looking girl?'

'Not Aurelia. The aunt. She thinks Bacon wrote Shakespeare.'

'Thinks who wrote what?' asked Archibald, puzzled, for the names were strange to him.

'You must have heard of Shakespeare. He's well known. Fellow who used to write plays. Only Aurelia's aunt says he didn't. She maintains that a bloke called Bacon wrote them for him.'

'Dashed decent of him,' said Archibald, approvingly. 'Of course, he may have owed Shakespeare money.'

'There's that, of course.'

'What was the name again?'

'Bacon.'

'Bacon,' said Archibald, jotting it down on his cuff. 'Right.'

Algy moved on, and Archibald, his soul bubbling within him like a welsh rabbit at the height of its fever, sank into a chair and stared sightlessly at the ceiling. Then, rising, he went off to the Burlington Arcade to buy socks.

The process of buying socks eased for awhile the turmoil that ran riot in Archibald's veins. But even socks with lavender clocks can only alleviate: they do not cure. Returning to his rooms, he found the anguish rather more overwhelming than ever. For at last he had leisure to think: and thinking always hurt his head.

Algy's careless words had confirmed his worst suspicions. A girl with an aunt who knew all about Shakespeare and Bacon must of necessity live in a mental atmosphere into which a lame-brained bird like himself could scarcely hope to soar. Even if he did meet her − even if she asked him to call − even if in due time their relations became positively cordial, what then? How could he aspire to such a goddess? What had he to offer her?

Money?

Plenty of that, yes, but what was money?

Socks?

Of these he had the finest collection in London, but socks are not everything.

A loving heart?

A fat lot of use that was.

No, a girl like Aurelia Cammarleigh would, he felt, demand from the man who aspired to her hand something in the nature of gifts, of accomplishments. He would have to be a man who Did Things.

And what, Archibald asked himself, could he do? Absolutely nothing except give an imitation of a hen laying an egg.

That he could do. At imitating a hen laying an egg he was admittedly a master. His fame in that one respect had spread all over the West End of London. 'Others abide our question. Thou art free,' was the verdict of London's gilded youth on Archibald Mulliner when considered purely in the light of a man who could imitate a hen laying an egg. 'Mulliner,' they said to one another, 'may be a pretty minus quantity in many ways, but he can imitate a hen laying an egg.'

And, so far from helping him, this one accomplishment of his would, reason told him, be a positive handicap. A girl like Aurelia Cammarleigh would simply be sickened by such coarse buffoonery. He blushed at the very thought of her ever learning that he was capable of sinking to such depths.

And so, when some weeks later he was introduced to her in the paddock at Ascot and she, gazing at him with what seemed to his sensitive mind contemptuous loathing, said:

'They tell me you give an imitation of a hen laying an egg, Mr Mulliner.'

He replied with extraordinary vehemence:

'It is a lie – a foul and contemptible lie which I shall track to its source and nail to the counter.'

Brave words! But had they clicked? Had she believed him? He trusted so. But her haughty eyes were very penetrating. They seemed to pierce through to the depths of his soul and lay it bare for what it was – the soul of a hen-imitator.

However, she did ask him to call. With a sort of queenly, bored disdain and only after he had asked twice if he might – but she did it. And Archibald resolved that, no matter what the mental strain, he would show her that her first impression of him had been erroneous; that, trivial and vapid though he might seem, there were in his nature deeps whose existence she had not suspected.

For a young man who had been superannuated from Eton and believed everything he read in the Racing Expert's column in the morning paper, Archibald, I am bound to admit, exhibited in this crisis a sagacity for which few of his intimates would have given him credit. It may be that love stimulates the mind, or it may be that when the moment comes Blood will tell. Archibald, you must remember, was, after all, a Mulliner: and now the old canny strain of the Mulliners came out in him.

'Meadowes, my man,' he said to Meadowes, his man.

'Sir,' said Meadowes.

'It appears,' said Archibald, 'that there is − or was − a cove of the name of Shakespeare. Also a second cove of the name of Bacon. Bacon wrote plays, it seems, and Shakespeare went and put his own name on the programme and copped the credit.'

'Indeed, sir?'

'If true, not right, Meadowes.'

'Far from it, sir.'

'Very well, then. I wish to go into this matter carefully. Kindly pop out and get me a book or two bearing on the business.'

He had planned his campaign with infinite cunning. He knew that, before anything could be done in the direction of winning the heart of Aurelia Cammarleigh, he must first establish himself solidly with the aunt. He must court the aunt, ingratiate himself with her − always, of course, making it clear from the start that she was not the one. And, if reading about Shakespeare and Bacon could do it, he would, he told himself, have her eating out of his hand in a week.

Meadowes returned with a parcel of forbidding-looking volumes, and Archibald put in a fortnight's intensive study. Then, discarding the monocle which had up till then been his constant companion, and substituting for it a pair of horn-rimmed spectacles which gave him something of the look of an earnest sheep, he set out for Park Street to pay his first call. And within five minutes of his arrival he had declined a cigarette on the plea that he was a non-smoker, and had managed to say some rather caustic things about the practice, so prevalent among his contemporaries, of drinking cocktails.

Life, said Archibald, toying with his teacup, was surely given to us for some better purpose than the destruction of our brains and digestions with alcohol. Bacon, for instance, never took a cocktail in his life, and look at him.

At this, the aunt, who up till now had plainly been regarding him as just another of those unfortunate incidents, sprang to life.

'You admire Bacon, Mr Mulliner?' she asked eagerly.

And, reaching out an arm like the tentacle of an octopus, she drew him into a corner and talked about Cryptograms for forty-seven minutes by the drawing-room clock. In short, to sum the thing up, my nephew Archibald, at his initial meeting with the only relative of the girl he loved, went like a sirocco. A Mulliner is always a Mulliner. Apply the acid test, and he will meet it.

It was not long after this that he informed me that he had sown the good seed to such an extent that Aurelia's aunt had invited him to pay a long visit to her country house, Brawstead Towers, in Sussex.

He was seated at the Savoy bar when he told me this, rather feverishly putting himself outside a Scotch and soda: and I was perplexed to note that his face was drawn and his eyes haggard.

'But you do not seem happy, my boy,' I said.

'I'm not happy.'

'But surely this should be an occasion for rejoicing. Thrown together as you will be in the pleasant surroundings of a country house, you ought easily to find an opportunity of asking this girl to marry you.'

'And a lot of good that will be,' said Archibald moodily.

'Even if I do get a chance I shan't be able to make any use of it. I wouldn't have the nerve. You don't seem to realize what it means being in love with a girl like Aurelia. When I look into those clear, soulful eyes, or see that perfect profile bobbing about on the horizon, a sense of my unworthiness seems to slosh me amidships like some blunt instrument. My tongue gets entangled with my front teeth, and all I can do is stand there feeling like a piece of Gorgonzola that has been condemned by the local sanitary inspector. I'm going to Brawstead Towers, yes, but I don't expect anything to come of it. I know exactly what's going to happen to me. I shall just buzz along through life, pining dumbly, and in the end slide into the tomb a blasted, blighted bachelor. Another whisky, please, and jolly well make it a double.'

Brawstead Towers, situated as it is in the pleasant Weald of Sussex, stands some fifty miles from London: and Archibald, taking the trip easily in his car, arrived there in time to dress comfortably for dinner. It was only when he reached the drawing-room at eight o'clock that he discovered that the younger members of the house-party had gone off in a body to dine and dance at a hospitable neighbour's, leaving him to waste the evening tie of a lifetime, to the composition of which he had devoted no less than twenty-two minutes, on Aurelia's aunt.

Dinner in these circumstances could hardly hope to be an unmixedly exhilarating function. Among the things which helped to differentiate it from a Babylonian orgy was the fact that, in deference to his known prejudices, no wine was served to Archibald. And, lacking artificial stimulus, he found the aunt even harder to endure philosophically than ever.

Archibald had long since come to a definite decision that

what this woman needed was a fluid ounce of weed-killer, scientifically administered. With a good deal of adroitness he contrived to head her off from her favourite topic during the meal: but after the coffee had been disposed of she threw off all restraint. Scooping him up and bearing him off into the recesses of the west wing, she wedged him into a corner of a settee and began to tell him all about the remarkable discovery which had been made by applying the Plain Cipher to Milton's well-known Epitaph on Shakespeare.

'The one beginning "What needs my Shakespeare for his honoured bones?"' said the aunt.

'Oh, that one?' said Archibald.

'"What needs my Shakespeare for his honoured bones? The labour of an Age in pilèd stones? Or that his hallowed Reliques should be hid under a starry-pointing Pyramid?"' said the aunt.

Archibald, who was not good at riddles, said he didn't know.

'As in the Plays and Sonnets,' said the aunt, 'we substitute the name equivalents of the figure totals.'

'We do what?'

'Substitute the name equivalents of the figure totals.'

'The which?'

'The figure totals.'

'All right,' said Archibald. 'Let it go. I daresay you know best.'

The aunt inflated her lungs.

'These figure totals,' she said, 'are always taken out in the Plain Cipher, A equalling one to Z equals twenty-four. The names are counted in the same way. A capital letter with the figures indicates an occasional variation in the Name Count. For instance, A equals twenty-seven, B twenty-eight, until K equals ten is reached, when K, instead of ten, becomes one, and T instead of nineteen, is one, and R or Reverse, and so on, until

A equals twenty-four is reached. The short or single Digit is not used here. Reading the Epitaph in the light of this Cipher, it becomes: "What need Verulam for Shakespeare? Francis Bacon England's King be hid under a W. Shakespeare? William Shakespeare. Fame, what needst Francis Tudor, King of England? Francis. Francis W. Shakespeare. For Francis thy William Shakespeare hath England's King took W. Shakespeare. Then thou our W. Shakespeare Francis Tudor bereaving Francis Bacon Francis Tudor such a tomb William Shakespeare."'

The speech to which he had been listening was unusually lucid and simple for a Baconian, yet Archibald, his eye catching a battle-axe that hung on the wall, could not but stifle a wistful sigh. How simple it would have been, had he not been a Mulliner and a gentleman, to remove the weapon from its hook, spit on his hands, and haul off and dot this doddering old ruin one just above the imitation pearl necklace. Placing his twitching hands underneath him and sitting on them, he stayed where he was until, just as the clock on the mantelpiece chimed the hour of midnight, a merciful fit of hiccoughs on the part of his hostess enabled him to retire. As she reached the twenty-seventh 'hic', his fingers found the door-handle and a moment later he was outside, streaking up the stairs.

Also available in Arrow

Joy in the Morning

P.G. Wodehouse

A Jeeves and Wooster novel

Trapped in rural Steeple Bumpleigh, a man less stalwart than
Bertie Wooster would probably give way at the knees.

For among those present were Florence Craye, to whom Bertie
had once been engaged and her new fiancé 'Stilton'
Cheesewright, who sees Bertie as a snake in the grass. And that
biggest blot on the landscape, Edwin the Boy Scout, who is busy
doing acts of kindness out of sheer malevolence.

All Bertie's forebodings are fully justified. For in his efforts to
oil the wheels of commerce, promote the course of true love
and avoid the consequences of a vendetta, he becomes the prey
of all and sundry. In fact only Jeeves can save him...

arrow books

Also available in Arrow

The Clicking of Cuthbert

P.G. Wodehouse

A Golf collection

The Oldest Member knows everything that has ever happened
on the golf course – and a great deal more besides.

Take the story of Cuthbert, for instance. He's helplessly in love
with Adeline, but what use are his holes in one when she's in thrall
to Culture and prefers rising young writers to winners of the
French Open? But enter a Great Russian Novelist with a strange
passion, and Cuthbert's prospects are transformed. Then look at
what happens to young Mitchell Holmes, who misses short putts
because of the uproar of the butterflies in the adjoining meadows.
His career seems on the skids – but can golf redeem it?

The kindly but shrewd gaze of the Oldest Member picks out
some of the funniest stories Wodehouse ever wrote.

arrow books

The P G Wodehouse Society (UK)

The P G Wodehouse Society (UK) was formed in 1997 to promote the enjoyment of the writings of the twentieth century's greatest humorist. The Society publishes a quarterly magazine, *Wooster Sauce*, which includes articles, features, reviews, and current Society news. Occasional special papers are also published. Society events include regular meetings in central London, cricket matches and a formal biennial dinner, along with other activities. The Society actively supports the preservation of the Berkshire pig, a rare breed, in honour of the incomparable Empress of Blandings.

MEMBERSHIP ENQUIRIES

Membership of the Society is open to applicants from all parts of the world. The cost of a year's membership in 2008 is £15. Enquiries and requests for membership forms should be made to the Membership Secretary, The P G Wodehouse Society (UK), 26 Radcliffe Rd, Croydon, Surrey, CRO 5QE, or alternatively from info@pgwodehousesociety.org.uk

The Society's website can be viewed at
www.pgwodehousesociety.org.uk

Visit our special P.G. Wodehouse website
www.wodehouse.co.uk

Find out about P.G. Wodehouse's books now
reissued with appealing new covers

Read extracts from all your favourite titles

Read the exclusive extra content and immerse
yourself in Wodehouse's world

Sign up for news of future publications
and upcoming events

arrow books